BLOOD
—OF THE—
WITNESS TREE

By

J.C. Vande Zande

MONTAG

First Montag Press E-Book and Paperback Original Edition October 2025

Copyright © 2025 by Jeff Vande Zande

Montag Press ISBN: 978-1-957010-60-1
Design © 2025 Amit Dey

Montag Press Team:

Cover: Rick Febre
Editor: Charlie Franco
Managing Director: Charlie Franco
Author Photo: Matt Brown

A Montag Press Book
www.montagpress.com
Montag Press
777 Morton Street, Unit B
San Francisco CA 94129 USA

Montag Press, the burning book with the hatchet cover, the skewed word mark and the portrayal of the long-suffering fireman mascot are trademarks of Montag Press.

Printed & Digitally Originated in the United States of America

10 9 8 7 6 5 4 3 2 1

"Pigeon River Country. It's big, it's wild, and it's quiet. There's magic in it. Things happen here that happen nowhere else."

Pigeon River Forest Discovery Center

CHAPTER 1

The high winds and torrential downpour descended on the forest like a vengeful demon summoned out of the void. The arrival of the violent weather had been in none of the television or radio forecasts even from as recent as that morning. They had all predicted the same thing: overcast all day with a high of 78 degrees.

They couldn't have been more wrong.

An hour or so before the storm struck, Nate Collins, a summer intern with the DNR's Discovery Center, had gone into the village of Vanderbilt to the west. Finding a cell signal in the Pigeon River Forest was nearly impossible, so he made up an excuse at least once a day to drive into town to text or call his girlfriend. He checked his phone's home screen. August 15. It was getting to be the slow time of the outdoors season, the dog days as they say. The morel mushroom hunters had long since come and gone. Near the end of June, when most of the significant insect hatches were over, many fishermen traded in their fly rods for golf clubs. People still camped, but not in the numbers they did in the spring and early summer when they were sloughing off the melancholy of winter. Nate's attention had already turned towards the coming semester back down in East Lansing. His girlfriend had spent the summer in Chicago with her parents. They'd only seen each other for a few days around the Fourth of July. He was looking forward to seeing her more regularly. The calm skies he drove beneath belied the colossal storm that would soon assault the forest.

Returning from Vanderbilt, Nate was going to turn left on Twin Lakes Road back toward the Discovery Center and headquarters, but Branson Strang, the head ranger, radioed him. Strang was Nate's favorite. Of the other two rangers, Dan Larsen was tolerable enough. Something about Dietrick Cross made Nate uneasy, like the man should have been a mortician but somehow ended up working as a ranger in a state forest. Nate had brought it up once to Strang, jokingly, but ever the diplomat, Strang had said, "Dietrick's all right. Just different. You never know someone's experiences. I try not to judge." The upshot message was, "and you shouldn't either."

Over the CB, Strang told him to check on the guy with the fifth wheel camper in the Sturgeon Valley Road rustic site. "I tried to get Luke to do it, but he's not answering his radio." Strang wanted to get a sense of how much longer the guy planned to stay. "Remind him it's a 15-night limit. The guy thinks he's got his own seasonal site up there or something."

When Nate arrived, the fifth wheel was gone. A rectangle of yellowed, withering grass marked where it had been. He parked the truck and walked around the site. The guy hadn't left that long ago. Some sticks of firewood lay in a haphazard pile. They would be scavenged by some other camper before long. A few burned-down logs were still smoldering in the fire pit. Weak wisps of smoke wandered skyward from the blackened wood. Nate poured the last of his water bottle over the most active embers.

As he made ready to climb back into the truck, a darkness poured across the overcast sky like someone spilling used motor oil over a garage floor. The trees bucked and plunged in the sudden downburst. Nate scrambled for the inside of the truck and watched the downpour turn the windshield into an opaque waterfall. The hammering rain was deafening. The truck rocked back and forth as though surrounded by rioters trying to get at some infamous dictator inside. With his left hand, Nate kept a death's grip on the grab handle above the driver's side door. His right palm pressed into the dashboard, bracing the rest of his body against the seat. It felt at times as though the wind was going to lift the truck right from the ground.

And then, as unexpectedly as it had started, the storm receded to the north-west. Nate could still hear some of the high-pitched, frightened noises that had come out of him while in the climax of the squall. He was glad none of the other interns had heard them. He wouldn't have heard the end of it, especially from Luke.

His pounding heart was finally starting to slow when Ranger Strang's voice came over the radio. "You all right, Collins?"

Nate picked up the CB. "Yeah, but that was a helluva wind." He cleared his throat and dropped his voice an octave. "Trails are going to be a mess."

"Agreed. We've got some good-sized trees down here. Looks like one went right through the roof of one of the cabins. Nobody hurt as far as I know."

"I can head back and help with cleanup. Chainsaws in the back of the truck are still ready to go after those downed trees we took out of the Pigeon last week."

"Negative. I need you to head over to Town Corner Lake. Dietrick and Luke might already be there, but I can't get them on the radio. We've got an occupied site over there. Gotta check to make sure everyone is okay. I haven't gotten a word yet on whether or not a tornado touched down somewhere in the forest. That wind was something."

"Isn't there someone camping over in the dispersed site on the Black?" Nate asked.

"Yeah," Strang confirmed. "A dad and his boy. I talked to the father yesterday. Check on them too, will ya? And let me know the condition of the roads."

Nate confirmed that he would go check out the campgrounds. He started the truck, backed out onto the road, and headed east. The gravel was wet and rutted in spots, but easily passable in the truck. Water dripped from the leaves, and a scattering of fallen branches was stitched over the road. Glancing to his left, he surveyed the two-track road that declined towards the Witness Tree. The pathway looked untouched. He knew from a class he'd taken that witness trees were often present during significant historical events, like George Washington's Mt. Vernon tree, which "witnessed" Washington's life. As far as he knew, the Witness Tree in the

Pigeon River State Forest was marked during the original land survey of Michigan.

Not much of a witnessing.

He rolled up and down the hills of Sturgeon Valley Road. A tree was down in the parking area at the Elk Viewing turnout. Someone would have to cut that up, but it probably wouldn't be him. He'd be back in East Lansing long before they'd be finished cleaning up after this storm. The state would probably have to bring in a special crew to get things back in shape. He turned on the radio. None of the stations mentioned the storm. Had it been that isolated? He wondered if maybe the rest of the forest had been untouched. At the t-intersection with Tin Shanty Bridge Road, he turned right and got his answer.

The driving was suddenly much harder to navigate, but the trees that had come down only partially blocked the road. He was able to work his way around the crowns and crunch his way over the scattered branches. He climbed out a few times to drag larger branches off to the shoulder. He figured that if he interned again the next summer, he'd probably spend most of it cleaning up the residual mess of this storm. Glancing into the depths of the woods that flanked either side of him revealed dozens of freshly downed trees, and that was just what he could see from the road. He couldn't even begin to imagine the condition of all the hiking and cross-country ski trails. "What a mess," he mumbled.

Looking into the woods again, he spotted a flash of gray. After a moment, the gray became an animal running at a high speed through the trees some fifty feet back into the woods.

It weaved through the standing trunks and jumped over the fallen. It ran like a dog but was too big to be a coyote. Hell, it was too big to be a deer. For a moment, he thought he saw antlers, but it was too brief for him to be certain. It had to be an elk, but the fully gray coat made that hard to imagine. The long, white tail certainly wasn't an elk feature either. After another moment, the animal was gone from his sight, disappeared into the trees and distance. He made a mental note to ask Ranger Strang what kind of animal it could be. He wondered if maybe it had something to do with the "massive feral dog" a few campers had reported spotting over the course of the summer. Shaking off a chill that snaked up his spine, he turned his attention back to the road.

After 25 minutes of steering around fallen limbs, he turned left onto Chandler Dam Road. Not more than a couple hundred yards along his way, he spotted trees down across his path. He knew immediately there would be no driving around them. He rolled closer, and the extent of the impasse became clear. It could only be described as a wall of trees, at least three or four feet high. He pulled up within ten feet and studied the barricade through the windshield. He shook his head. The trees didn't lay haphazard but instead were braided around each other. In his Michigan Flora and Fauna class, they'd learned about bittersweet vine, an invasive species that coils around other trees and shrubs, often girdling their victims until nutrients can't flow through the constricted limbs, eventually killing them.

This wasn't bittersweet vine, though. It was white pine, valued as lumber for how straight it grows, and red pine, twisted around each other tight like pretzels. He couldn't imagine trying to chainsaw through it. It made no sense. No wind was strong enough to turn mature pine trunks into corkscrews. It looked as though it were done by design.

He picked up the radio. "Ranger Strang? You available?"

"Strang stepped out," Ranger Larsen answered. "What do you need, Nate?"

Nate depressed the button on his microphone. "When you see him, tell him I didn't get anywhere near Town Corner Lake or the dispersed site. There are trees down over Chandler Dam Road. I've never seen anything like it." He described the twisted trees.

Dan Larsen was quiet for a moment. Then: "How deep is it?"

"Do you mean high?"

"No, deep. How much of the road does it cover?"

Nate nodded to himself. "Okay, gotcha. Hold on a second." He got out of the truck and climbed up onto the hood. A cold steady breeze blew out of the forest, making him shiver. Looking ahead of him, he swallowed and then whistled in disbelief.

What amounted to nearly half a football field of trees lay in front of him, covering the road like a thick runner rug woven from timber.

They wouldn't get through it for weeks.

CHAPTER 2

There was no mistaking the sound of the small body stunning itself against the windowpane. Isaac Fletcher heard the strike while kneeling next to his lawn mower, untwisting the gas cap. He winced involuntarily, having heard the sound here and there throughout his life. Craning his neck, he examined the guestroom window at the back of the house. With the sharp noise the collision had made, he guessed that there might be a splintering of cracks. Seeing none, he exhaled a sigh of relief. Off to the right of the window's dead center, the bird's impact had left a greasy smudge of gray and a single feather. Though too small to be from one, it was black like a raven feather. Isaac's mind started to careen toward old memories, toward the worst night of his life, the worst year. It was over a decade ago. He had almost lost his daughter to what he could only guess was some kind of satanic ritual. His brother brutally murdered. But first, in January of that year, that damn raven flying straight into their windshield, blinding him. The car spinning over the black ice and into the trees.

His wife Gwen's startled scream from the passenger seat, and then total silence...

Through popping knees, Isaac pushed himself to standing. His femur echoed pain along its fault line of the long-ago inflicted injury of that car accident. The bone ached in cold weather. He would always have the metal inside of him, a constant reminder of...

Not going there, he thought. The dark places his mind could wander often left him immobile, staring off into nothingness.

He'd waited for years for the vivid memories to diminish, like snowbanks receding in the spring. No such luck. Instead, he'd learned that he needed to distract himself when the images came rushing into his mind.

The window. Just focus on the window.

He recalled reading somewhere that birds flew into windows because they were tricked by the reflection of the trees and the sky in the glass. They'd fly into it as though it offered any other distant horizon. An invisible reality struck them right between the eyes.

In the corner of the yard, the black, blue, red, and yellow of Carson's archery target caught Isaac's eye. He had helped his son position it so if an arrow did go over the fence it would go into a small stand of trees, not a neighbor's yard. Most of the neighbors were older and barely ventured onto their back lawns. The chance of hitting someone was negligible.

The way Carson was shooting, it was unlikely that he would miss the target anyway, let alone send a stray over the shadowbox fence. When Carson was thirteen, Isaac had helped him get his Base Apprentice License so he could bow hunt for deer under Isaac's supervision. He still kicked himself for starting his son too young. It was too vulnerable of an age for him to declare, "Hunting sucks," and then believe it for the rest of his life. The quiet repose of hunting, especially hunting from a tree stand, was more suited to someone with some years under their belt. With age came the desire for hours of peaceful reflection.

For a freshly minted teenager? Not so much.

Isaac had watched Carson play different video games on his computer, and the damn things practically looked as good as watching a movie. They'd come a long way since Pong and Space Invaders. How could something as dull as waiting for a buck or a doe to appear possibly compete?

Somewhere in the neighborhood someone started a mower. Isaac traced a fingernail absently through his eyebrow, still recalling the botched attempt at turning Carson into a hunter.

After their first weekend of hunting some public land north of Midland, they'd returned the next weekend. They'd discovered that someone had stolen their tree stand. "That two-person stand was probably a little too tempting to the wrong personality type," Isaac had said. He wasn't surprised when, shivering in his camouflage pants and hoodie, Carson announced, "That's alright. I really don't think deer hunting is for me." Isaac had chalked it up to yet another one of those disappointments that come with parenthood.

Disappointed or not, Isaac was surprised when the bow hunting went by the wayside, but not the archery. Carson continued to practice with his compound bow even after he'd made his feelings known about deer hunting. The target in the corner of the backyard had two practice arrows sticking out of the outer yellow ring and one right in the bullseye. It irked Isaac that Carson wasn't hearing him when he said he needed to put his arrows away. Still, he couldn't help but be impressed by his son's accuracy. Carson had never shown much interest in sports, so it pleased Isaac that in October, they'd be driving down to the Flint Bowman Club for Carson to compete in a youth archery tournament.

They had a fly-fishing trip coming up in the next few days, and Carson had asked if he could bring his bow, the target, and the target stand. Isaac agreed instantly, relieved that his son wasn't trying to bring along anything with a screen. He hoped he could get Carson to warm up to fly fishing much more than he had deer hunting. Since his retirement two years ago, it had been a dream of Isaac's to have his son as a regular fishing partner.

He glanced in the direction of the bedroom window again but saw no movement on the ground. With luck, the bird had either flown away or was just stunned. Isaac hoped that he wouldn't be dealing with an injured animal. Mercy killing or no, it was never fun. He stared again absently at the archery target, letting his mind wander.

He and Carson had tried some fly fishing earlier that summer on the South Branch of the Au Sable just downstream from the Fisherman's Chapel. Even with accessibility limited to two-track roads, the stretch was heavily fished, so when he and Carson did catch trout, they were exclusively dinks and fingerlings. The one better-sized fish that Carson caught, about ten inches, turned out to be a large creek chub. He had slipped it into his creel so quickly and proudly that Isaac waited nearly 30 minutes before he had the heart to tell him that it wasn't even a trout: "It's a garbage fish, pal." With obvious disappointment, Carson had tossed it into the river and watched the body float downstream.

Then, in early August, Isaac had a vivid dream of when he was in his thirties and used to fish the Black River north of Gaylord in the Pigeon River Forest. In the dream, he was pulling in 10, 15, and 20-inch brook trout with each cast. It was the exact opposite of a nightmare. He seldom remembered his dreams, but he had woken with that one replaying in his mind throughout the day, daring him to ignore its promise of big trout. Goaded by the dream, he planned a three-day fly-fishing trip, including camping, cooking over a fire, and enjoying the woods when not out on the water. He remembered the perfect rustic camping site right on the river. If this trip didn't win Carson over to the beauty of fly fishing and the outdoorsman's life, then probably nothing would.

We leave in a couple days, Isaac thought, smiling. Turning away from the archery target, he started for the guestroom side of the house, making a mental note to jot down a list of everything they'd need for the upcoming trip.

"Dad, what was that..that *noise?*"

Emily.

Isaac felt his nerves tighten. Sometimes her anxiety seemed to be getting worse by the day.

He glanced at her on the back porch with her pale, expectant face pressed against the screen. She was wearing pajama pants and a shirt with some kind of cartoon characters flanked by Japanese words. His mind did a quick calculation, and his left eye twitched. "Wait, what...? Weren't you supposed to be at work over an hour ago?"

Emily pushed her fingers through her short hair. Two weeks before, it had been long, almost down to the middle of her back, but on a whim she and her girlfriend had decided to cut each other's hair. The resulting hairstyles looked ideal for a six or seven-year-old boy. "I called in," she said. She looked down into the floor of the porch before making eye contact with him again.

"Wha... why this time?" He regretted the words immediately, and the biting tone in which he'd delivered them.

Emily's pleading look into his eyes was all she had to give. It was a look that said, "Dad, I don't know any other way to explain anxiety to you. I've tried, but you just don't seem to listen, or care. It's not anything I'm doing on purpose."

He shrugged one of his hands into the air. "I mean, it's a daycare. It's just, with them watching people's kids like that, it's probably tough for them to manage when someone calls in. Don't they have to have a certain ratio of adults to kids? You don't want to lose that job." Did it really matter? On a good week, she might work fifteen hours.

"They already got someone to cover for her." A young woman's voice, seemingly disembodied, came out of the corner of the porch near the sliding glass door where the siding of the house met the edge of one of the screened walls. Wearing all black, she was almost invisible wedged into the shadowed right angle. "They're pretty understanding," she said. Her emphasis of "they're" carried with it the sentiment "unlike you," a not-so-subtle indictment of Isaac's apparent insensitivity.

Harper.

She and Emily had met the past winter in an art class at the local community college. It was one of only three classes that Emily had finished with a passing grade. The other dozen courses or so that she'd attempted over the years after high school, she'd either dropped or just stopped attending and failed. Going to classes in person triggered her social anxiety. Taking online classes required a self-directedness that she didn't possess. Harper at least gave her someone in her life. They seemed to have a lot in common, which included working on a graphic novel together that Harper was writing and Emily drawing.

Unlike Emily, Harper could at least drive, and that skill had taken the pressure off Isaac to get Emily to work when she did work. Both she and Harper presented as much younger, and he had a hard time seeing their relationship as anything but platonic, though he guessed that wasn't the case. Ever since college had let out for the summer, Harper spent most of her free time at Emily's. Well, at *my* house, Isaac thought. He wondered if his youngest daughter would ever strike out on her own. Ashley, his eldest, sometimes got on him about trying online dating. He just couldn't see a woman being interested in someone who had an almost twenty-two-year-old at home who functioned like she was twelve.

I was too soft with her, Isaac lamented. He turned on himself almost instantly. But what am I supposed to do? The world is just too much for her. He scratched his chin absently. "Well, just clean up the kitchen if you two end up making anything to eat," he said.

"Dad? What *was* that noise?"

He closed his eyes and squeezed his forehead between the fingers and thumb of his left hand. Taking his hand away, he opened his eyes. He knew what was coming. He could delay her exaggerated response but wouldn't be able to stop it. "Just a bird. Must have flown into the guestroom window," he said as casually as he could.

"Where is it? Is it okay? Can it fly?" Emily moved to the screen that looked out toward the guestroom side of the yard. Her eyes searched the ground frantically.

Oh boy. He held up a yielding palm. "Hun, I haven't even looked yet. I'm sure it's fine. Might have even flown away already. Usually, they're just stunned for a few minutes. You guys go ahead in, I'll let you know. I picked up more Pop-Tarts," he said, offering the last as what he hoped would be an irresistible temptation.

He turned toward the basement window well beneath the guestroom sill. Instead of hearing the sliding glass door close behind the girls as they went inside, he heard the screen door of the porch slam and Emily's quick footsteps shishing across the grass toward him. She arrived at his side and, as it often did, her height surprised him. She was nearly eye to eye with him as she shifted from one foot to the other. He could feel Harper's presence like a spider on the porch, pressed against the screen, watching them.

"Do you see it? Is it okay? Did it fly away? Is it okay?" Emily sounded like an auctioneer.

Turning toward her, he took her shoulders in his hands, a calming gesture he engaged in nearly every day. At least he guessed it was calming. "Emily, you need to take a breath. Like I said, it probably flew away or—"

"It's right there," Harper said, "near that bush."

Isaac and Emily's eyes followed her pointing finger to the rose bush that he had planted for Gwen almost two decades prior. There was something off with the soil because the bush had never in all its years bloomed. Not far from the bush, a juvenile mourning dove's body shimmied around a twisted wing.

Isaac caught his hand around Emily's upper arm as she lurched involuntarily toward the bird. "Hun, it's got a broken wing." Emily's skinny arm jerking back against his grip was stronger than he would have guessed. "You and Harper just need to go inside."

"Dad, let me go! I need to help it!"

He wondered what his neighbors were thinking of her histrionics. He took a deep breath and exhaled it. "Emily, I need you to calm down." Having had a little longer to look, he guessed that the bird also had a broken leg.

"You shouldn't grab someone like that."

Harper's tone suggested Isaac was doing something nefarious by keeping his daughter from adding to the bird's pain. In their eyes, he could do nothing right. His gas-guzzling truck was killing the environment. His non-organic groceries were poisoning their bodies, even as they consumed some of the worst fast-food he could imagine. His desperate, short-sighted clinging to the "capitalist system" was only feeding a cornered dragon that would devour them all.

A feeling, angry and justified, crept up the back of his neck. He pulled back on Emily's arm and then, turning, positioned himself between her and the wounded animal. "Girls, this isn't..." He pointed his free hand behind him, but kept his eyes locked on Emily's. "That bird is not going to make it, no matter what you do. You just need to go inside. Now."

Emily wrenched at his grip, but he kept his hand clamped around her wrist.

"Dad, let go! Let me go! You don't understand." She was working herself into a lather.

"Let her go," Harper demanded.

Jesus Christ. At this point, he wouldn't have been surprised if his neighbors called the police. Isaac released Emily's wrist, but just as quickly clamped her shoulders between his hands. "Look at me." He gave her a small shake and repeated his demand.

She stopped her convulsing and glared into his eyes. Her own were red and tear brimmed. Her breaths were ragged, but she kept a steady, determined gaze on his.

"Listen, that bird is suffering. It's going to suffer to death, which could take hours. It needs to be put out of its—"

"No!"

With the sides of her thumbs pressed together, Emily thrust her palms and splayed fingers into Isaac's chest. Hands ripped from her shoulders, he stumbled backwards and then fell onto the ground. He gasped short, shallow breaths. His ribs tingled painfully, not unlike the feeling of walking on a foot that has fallen asleep. Struggling to get a full breath, he propped himself up on his elbows. He rubbed the back of his head where it had struck the ground. With her back to him, Emily kneeled, blocking his view of the young mourning dove.

"Em— don't—" It's all he could manage with the wind so recently knocked from him. He tried for a deeper breath, but it too was stopped short. It was as though a hulking man had shoved him to the ground and not a skinny twenty-one-year-old girl.

Holding her hands cupped over the bird, Emily turned on her knees towards the rest of the backyard. She whispered into the space between her thumbs. The bird's small head and beady eyes peeked out between her fingers.

Isaac barely discerned her whispered mantra at the edges of his hearing: "You're okay. You're okay. You're okay." When she opened her hands, the bird took to flight in an explosion of flapping. It landed in a nearby maple tree.

Blinking, Isaac studied the bird where it perched on a branch. Like him, it seemed to be in stunned disbelief. It gave a long, ghostly coo and then flew off out of sight.

"Yes!" Harper shouted. "Yes!"

Isaac looked from where the bird had perched to his daughter. She kneeled just feet from him. Her face was drained of all color. "Em? You okay?"

She looked at him, smiled faintly, and then collapsed on the ground, eyes closed.

CHAPTER 3

With his phone pinned between his ear and shoulder, Isaac crouched on his knees on the concrete floor. The ache of it was almost unbearable. He reached under one of the basement shelves until his fingers found the plated steel.

"Are you okay? You sound like you're having a stroke," Ashley said on her end of the call.

"I'm fine. I'm fine," he grunted. He pulled the dust-covered grill grate from under the bottom shelf. He rested for a moment on hands and knees. "But back to what you were suggesting...I really don't know if I want to mess with marijuana."

She sighed. "Why not? It's not like it's illegal."

Isaac leaned the grate upright against the lowest shelf and then used the other shelves to hoist himself to his feet. His knees popped through their straightening. He exhaled. "I know it's legal now. Hell, I voted for that, even though it was never really my thing...here and there in high school mainly. Some in college." He massaged his knees. "I just worry about if it might somehow get me drinking again." He walked the grill grate to the pile of camping and fishing gear he was amassing in the middle of the basement floor.

Someone's footsteps creaked in the floor joists above him. It was either Emily or Harper getting something from the kitchen. The gait was too leisurely for Carson.

"Dad, it's called California sober. A lot of people do it. If weed was never your thing, and you never did it when you drank, I don't see how it could be a trigger."

"I suppose," he said. "I *am* getting desperate. I'm like a zombie some days." He'd explained to her that he'd tried several different sleep aids: Melatonin. Sominex. ZzzQuil. His doctor had tried to prescribe Ambien, but Isaac refused based on the side effects. The last time he'd tried it, over a decade ago, he'd had a horrific nightmare of Gwen and how she'd looked the night of their car accident. It wasn't a dream so much as a vivid reliving.

Never again.

"I mean, I've had the insomnia off and on for a decade," Isaac explained, "but this summer it's been really bad. If I'm here at the house and I don't fall asleep until six in the morning, I can just sleep in. It's no big deal." Scanning the top shelf, he spotted his cooler. "Or I can just take a long nap in the afternoon." Up on tiptoes, he pulled the cooler from the shelf by its handle. He set it on the floor. "But it's not like a nap will be an option when I have Carson with me up in a state forest. I'm going to need to get some sleep."

"If you get some gummies with CBN, I can almost guarantee you that you'll sleep. Just drive into Bay City. They have a ton of dispensaries."

A small magpie moth bumped against the dusk-lit pane of one of the basement windows. Sorry pal, Isaac thought, I can't let you out. Those hinges are rusted shut. The idea came to him that after the call with Ashley, he could catch the moth with a cup. Maybe he could tell Emily about it or even bring her outside with him to release it. She'd like that.

"I might just *have* to go to a dispensary," he said. "I've gotta get sleep."

"Well, at least just go get some edibles. You'll have them with you if you get desperate enough."

"I'll look into it." Using his foot, Isaac slid the cooler across the floor to join the rest of his camping gear. He was pretty sure he had most of it. At least enough of it that he could take a break. He sat down on the cooler and took the phone in his hand. He stretched a kink from his neck, took a long breath, and exhaled.

"If the gummies you get end up having THC, just make sure you get indica. I don't think you and a sativa strain would get along."

He rubbed his palm over his stubbly cheek. "You see, I don't remember it being so complicated. Back when I was messing around, when I was a teenager, it was just pot. You met some sketchy dude in a park, got in his car, and he traded your money for a baggie. That's it. The way you talk about it, it's like another language."

Ashley laughed. "All you have to tell them is that you want CBN gummies, and if they have THC in them, you want it to be pure indica, not hybrids. That's it."

He nodded. "Alright. Text that to me, if you don't mind."

She was quiet on her end. A moment later his phone chimed. His lock screen showed most of the text from her. How the hell did she thumb that in so quickly?

"Got it. Thanks." Above him, two sets up of footsteps pounded across the first level floor from the kitchen, through the living room, and into Emily's bedroom. The door slammed, and then he heard Harper playfully threatening that Emily better let her in. "I'll push you down right on your coccyx," Harper said, laughing. The door then creaked open on its hinges. They both started laughing. If he didn't know better, he would have guessed that two eleven-year-olds were having a sleepover. Why coccyx? Was it because the word almost sounded like profanity? Christ, they could be so juvenile. He sighed.

"You okay, Dad?"

With his thumb resting against his temple, he closed his eyes and massaged the tips of his fingers into the middle of his forehead. "I guess... What about you? How is everything with the baby? Going to be here soon. How's Ben?"

"Ben's good. Just busy with work. He's the new guy trying to prove himself and all that." She explained that everything was going well with her pregnancy. "I'm just really tired and ready for her to get here. The doctor likes everything she's seeing on the ultrasounds. She's going to be big. Not looking forward to that."

Isaac stood up and walked toward their fishing waders hanging, socks up, in the corner. "Are you still thinking of a natural birth? Your mom swore by those epidurals."

"Yeah, we're going natural."

He pulled a pair of the waders down and started toward the pile. "Well, at least have an epidural ordered. You'll have it if *you* get desperate enough," he said, teasingly echoing their earlier conversation about edibles.

"Very funny."

He draped the waders over the pile and then went back for the other pair. The moth was still fluttering around the window. "I'm just glad everything is going so well for you guys. I'll be heading your way soon enough once the baby gets here. I'm sorry it's been a while since I've gotten over to see you," Isaac said.

"We understand. Muskegon isn't an easy drive coming from that side of the state. And you've got your hands full too."

He lifted Carson's waders from their spot. "That's an understatement." Jesus, it shouldn't be a statement at all, he thought. Emily's twenty-one years old. How was it that her maturing was so stunted?

Just the night before, lying in the dark, he'd been suddenly consumed with the thought of bringing Emily along on the fishing trip. Harper could go too. He'd felt certain that it needed to happen. Sure, it would relieve any worry about leaving her alone at the house, but it was more than that. He had remembered reading somewhere that anxiety was on the rise in young people because they spent too much time isolated on screens. Maybe what Emily needed was to take her love of animals and expand it into a love of the outdoors. He'd lain in bed imagining she and Harper taking hikes, roasting marshmallows, and catching fireflies.

He'd almost woken Emily at two o'clock in the morning to tell her the new plan. Instead, he'd fallen to sleep and soon into a dream. In it, he was fishing with Emily on a stretch of the Pigeon River he'd fished many times in his youth. She was some 50 feet ahead of him casting to what he knew to be a deep spot. He watched her fly drift across the expanse of the hole. Coming up out of the surface, a water-rotted human hand grabbed her fly. Emily's rod doubled over with the weight of the sudden pulling. She turned to look back at Isaac, her face a portrait of panic as whatever was at the end of her line dragged her toward the hole.

"Just let go, Emily! Let go of the rod!" he shouted. His own feet were cemented into place where his wader boots had sunken down into the mud.

"Daddy!" she screamed. The water rose up her abdomen, over the top of her waders, and then up to her chin. More gray hands rose up out of the water all around her head, grabbing at her hair.

"Emily, let go!" He watched her face slip under. The water rushed into her open-mouthed scream.

He'd woken sweaty and with a racing heart. Even that, just the obvious simplicity of dropping the rod. She couldn't do it. It was hours before he fell asleep again. In the morning, the realities of having Emily, let alone Emily *and* Harper, on the trip dawned on him. Coyotes howling at night. Mosquitos feeding on them. Food cooked over a fire. They'd be scared and miserable and thereby everyone would be miserable. They liked their pajamas, overstuffed furniture, and snacks that slid easily in and then out of a microwave. No, he'd decided.

It was a trip about Carson. The kid deserved some time alone with his dad. Emily needed to stay home, anyway, so she could go to work.

Isaac started toward the fly rod cases leaning in a corner of the basement.

"How is Emily doing?" Ashley asked. "And don't just say 'fine.' You're not burdening me by talking about it. I know she's been frustrating."

He stopped, held the phone away from his ear, looked at it, and then brought it back to his ear. "When did you get so grown up?"

"Dad."

He pinched his nose a few times between his index finger and thumb. "What? I'm paying you a compliment." He sighed. "I don't know. The anxiety stuff...it's like she says, I just don't understand it. It's like a curse or something. I end up feeling sorry for her every time. And I just doubt myself and what I'm supposed to be doing." He told her about just days before when he was getting ready to euthanize the mourning dove with the flat side of a shovel. "You see, like there...I'm all cocksure about something, and then I'm dead wrong. Damn thing was just stunned."

"She passed out?"

He shrugged a hand into the air. "It was pretty high emotions. I think she was just overwhelmed. Everything seems like high emotions with those two. Especially Em."

Feet in socks jogged through the living room, then the kitchen, and stopped at the threshold at the top of the basement stairs. "Dad?" It was Carson. "Should I pack my Fluoxetine?"

Isaac moved the phone away from his mouth. "Are you supposed to take it every day?"

"Yeah."

Isaac scratched absently at his stubbled cheek. "Then what do you think?"

Ashley sniffed out a little laugh on her side of the call.

"But, we just picked up the refill. What if I lose it?"

"You're not going to— Look, just grab a sandwich bag from the kitchen and put three of your pills in it. Just pack that then."

Carson said nothing else. A drawer opened in the kitchen, crinkle of plastic, and then the drawer slid shut. His footsteps pounded off in the direction of his room.

Isaac put the phone back to his ear. "Fluoxetine." He shook his head. "Even that, we didn't have that when I was a kid. I just don't remember it being like that...kids all racked up with anxiety or depression or both. I just wonder—"

"I'm on an anti-depressant. At least I was before I got pregnant."

Isaac closed his eyes and squeezed his forehead with his free hand. "It sounds like I'm judging. I'm not. I'm just saying that it's tough for me to understand. So much of the stuff they're going through, stuff you went through, I never did. Like I never lost a parent when I was young. I mean, not that young, anyway." He walked to the corner and picked up Carson's rod case. "And when I was Emily's age, I was already in an apartment in East Lansing, over 100 miles from home, splitting bills with roommates." He leaned the rod case into the gear pile. "I was becoming an adult. You know, like you did when you went off to NMU. I wasn't living in my parents' house swooning over comic books." He picked up his own rod case and paced back toward the pile. "Hell, she's twenty-one years old and doesn't show the slightest interest in even learning how to drive, let alone getting an apartment."

Ashley was quiet for a moment on her end. "She told me that you told her that apartments aren't everything they're cracked up to be. She said you said an apartment would be a waste of money when she could live for free with you."

He swallowed and then cleared his throat. "Maybe I said that. I was probably just telling her there's no need to rush if she's not sure what she's doing. I just don't think she could handle it."

"Maybe not knowing what she's doing is what she needs to be doing. Maybe she just needs to get out there and try her hand at the world. You know, see how she handles it, poorly or not."

Isaac pinched again at his running nose. The dust he was kicking up in the basement was getting to him. "I don't know," he said. "Maybe."

"Do you think that maybe constantly hearing from you that she'll never grow up is maybe keeping her from growing up? Like maybe there's a part of you that doesn't want her to—"

"So, you're saying this is my fault."

"That's not what I'm saying. I'm just saying, we don't always know why we act the way we do. You went through a lot, and that can come out in counter-intuitive ways. What if you're afraid of—"

"Okay," he said, not caring for the direction of the conversation.

Ashley cleared her throat. "Don't take this wrong, okay?" She sniffed. "Ever consider that what you have with Emily might be a little co-dependent or—"

"Ash."

"Seriously, I just wonder if there's a part of you that doesn't want her to leave. You lost Mom. You lost Uncle Adam. You almost lost Emily once, so if you can always keep her in your house—"

"I do think about that sometimes," Isaac interrupted. "What I wonder about is if everything that happened at the cabin...like somehow she's carrying it and it's coming out as anxiety, like something she can't quite put her finger on eating away at her. Probably another reason that I can't pull the tough love act with her." He sat down on the cooler again. "That whole period...that whole year was crazy. It doesn't always feel like it really happened, but I know it did. You know it." He scratched at his thigh through his jeans. "She doesn't know it, though. Emily. She hardly remembers anything from that night. She remembers stuff we did around the cabin, then getting her period, and then staying at the hotel in Cheboygan. That's pretty much it. But that doesn't mean that she didn't go through it."

"Sometimes I remember more than I want to," Ashley said.

Isaac stretched out his left leg and massaged his thigh. The moth lay against the window. Its wings slowly closed into something like diminutive hands in prayer and then opened again. "With Emily," Isaac said. "I saw what was happening to her through the doorway of the bedroom. She was unconscious, but...I just wonder—"

"Hold on, Dad. I've got someone at the door. I'm sorry. I'll be right back."

Isaac sat on the cooler staring up at the ground-level window as the memories flooded his mind. He was vaguely aware of the moth fluttering again in frustration against the glass.

There had been Gwen's funeral, followed by the months of him floundering through trying to raise the kids on his own. He was drinking too much. Wanting to be a better father, he had the idea to take the kids to Orphan Island for Emily's eleventh birthday. His mother-in-law had come to the cabin to celebrate with them. And Adam, his brother, had come.

Adam...

Isaac put his hand over his mouth and breathed in sharply through his nose to hold back the tears. He cleared his throat forcefully.

Evelyn Cameron and Silas Jameson, the only other residents of Orphan Island, had tried to take Emily from him. More than a kidnapping, Emily's soul was to whither inside the crone's body, and conversely the old woman would get a fresh body, another youth, to keep living. They'd somehow poisoned Emily into unconsciousness. They'd kidnapped Adam, flayed him, and used his skin in their twisted ceremony.

His brother. They'd skinned his brother as though his were just any other animal carcass.

"Goddamn it," Isaac said under his breath into the chilled air of the basement. His hand squeezed his phone as though trying to crush it. He eased his grip.

Everything involved was a blur of unfathomable events. The unearthly storm. His savage fight with Silas. And then Evelyn, naked, laid out in a field under the full moon and a whorl of circling bats overhead. She'd lain under Adam's skin as though it were a blanket. With sweat dripping in his eyes, Isaac had plunged the syringe into her vein.

And then it was over.

Helen, Ashley, Carson...they were okay. Emily had woken up, confused, but alive and still herself.

They'd won, though the victory proved to be cold comfort given what they'd lost.

Not long after they'd left the island, Theresa, the woman with the dogs, waited for them at a bonfire on the nearby shore. The lights of the village of Witiko twinkled behind her. "I could feel that something was happening out there," she'd said, pointing toward the island. "It might not yet be over." They stayed at her fire only a short time. Leaving Theresa, they'd gone into Cheboygan, and the stay in the hotel there would be the beginning of slowly going back to normal life.

Of course, normal life first meant dealing with a police investigation. There had been no denying that Adam's car was still parked in the village of Witiko. There had been no denying that he was missing. And as the investigation had developed, nobody could deny that something bizarre and tragic had happened on Orphan Island during that heinous thunderstorm. Fortunately, there were enough missing pieces from the puzzle that the police never arrived at a definitive conclusion. No arrests had been made. The missing persons cases remained open.

Isaac looked up at the moth bumping frantically against the glass of the basement window. Soon, buddy, he thought. We'll get you out of here.

As the police had conducted their search, Isaac had waited for them to make the discovery of Adam's remains. They never found his skin, which Isaac guessed an animal might have dragged deeper into the swamp or simply consumed altogether. The bones though? Wouldn't they have found some trace of him in Silas's shed or workshop or wherever the hell he worked on his goddamn human pelts?

They'd searched for weeks but never turned up even one pinky bone from the three missing bodies, something Isaac couldn't understand but didn't press. He'd seen enough that night to know that his brother was gone. Any traces of the other two bodies would only serve to put Isaac in hot water. He never really put it in specific terms in his mind. He'd done what needed to be done with Silas and Evelyn, but if anyone else had witnessed it, they'd have called it murder.

With enough coaching beforehand, Carson answered every police question with either "I don't know" or "I don't remember." Isaac had told him that much of what he did remember was from a long, sleepwalking episode. A nightmare of sorts. Maybe it was psychological abuse, but Isaac always thought it better than a five-year-old trying to live with the horrific truth of what had happened.

When the police questioned him, Isaac had explained that Silas must have had some kind of panicked episode during the storm, a psychotic break or something. It was the only way to rationalize the obvious signs of an altercation in the cabin. Silas, Isaac told the police, had burst through the door, shouted incoherently, and then tripped and crashed through the coffee table before running out the back door. The only thing Isaac had been able to make out from Silas' rambling was something about Evelyn wandering out into the storm.

He remembered being thankful that there had been no mention of a polygraph test. He'd have failed.

As relieved as he'd been about the family being able to keep their stories straight, the island being free of any signs of suspicious activity brought him little comfort. Where were the bodies? At the very least, where were the bones? The storm certainly couldn't have washed everything away. The police couldn't have been that inept. And, still, as the weeks had passed, and even with a detective or two certain of foul play, the case slowly went cold.

That autumn after Emily's 11th birthday, after everything that had happened, the kids stayed with Helen on the weekends, a limited joint custody of sorts. Isaac was supposed to be using the weekends to grieve while also working on keeping his sobriety. He secretly relapsed a few times over those first months. He forgave himself, considering what he'd been through. The kids had lost Uncle Adam, but only Isaac carried the burden of what truly had happened to his brother. Not to mention, he was still grieving Gwen. He couldn't blame himself for slipping up a few times. By Christmas of that ugly year, he was done. For good. Hadn't touched a drop since.

A small, tinny voice interrupted his thoughts. It called to him: "Dad? Dad, are you still there?"

Isaac looked down at the phone in his hand resting against his knee. He blinked a few times bringing his eyes into focus. "Yeah," he said, switching the phone to speaker, "I'm here."

Ashley explained that she'd had a pizza delivery person at the door, but the kid had the wrong address. After some guesswork, she was able to redirect him to the right neighbor several houses down the street.

Isaac sighed. "Well, like I was saying, I just wonder if, you know, even with her not remembering, if that night did something to Emily, like made her too tender for the world or something."

Ashley sniffed in a breath. "From what I remember, she was always anxious. Always high strung." She cleared her throat. "Have you guys stopped with the psychiatrist?"

Isaac stood up from the cooler. He paced the basement, circling the pile of camping and fishing gear. "Shit, that was a mess. Everything they tried either had bad side effects, made her worse, or didn't do anything." He waved his hand through the air in front of him. "We've taken a break from trying medications."

"Well, it might be worth—"

"Thing I can't wrap my mind around is how is that something that even happened. How'd we go through something that crazy, that awful? How is that whole thing part of our past, and now here we are living normal lives?" He shook his head.

Ashley was quiet a moment. "When I did my social work internship, they had me working with veterans at the outpatient clinic in Marquette. You remember. I was mainly helping fill out intake questionnaires. Still, I'd hear parts of their stories. Much of it sounded worse than what we went through. So much death. Death of friends. Blown off limbs. Still, a lot of them, with the right therapist, get better. They put it behind them. It's possible."

Isaac stopped his pacing. "Is this about me? You think I should be in therapy?"

"I didn't say that. I just meant that people go through trauma, a lot of people, and they come out on the other side of it still grocery shopping, watching TV in the evenings, and worrying about their 401ks. Ours was just a unique trauma."

Isaac nodded thoughtfully but didn't say anything. Above him, two sets of feet padded toward the kitchen. He tapped down the volume on his phone.

"I just think it's probably for the best, in my professional opinion," Ashley continued, "not to focus on the past too much. You can't really do anything about what happened. You can only do what you can do right now. Like what you're doing with Carson...taking him camping and fishing. That's good. That'll be good for both of you."

Isaac looked at the gear and nodded. "I do worry about leaving Emily here alone." He shook his head. "But hearing myself say it? It's crazy. She's almost twenty-two years old. She will be twenty-two years old in less than a week." He shook his head again. "Hell, at fifteen you were practically raising your brother and sister. Remember?"

"Hey," Ashley started. "Saturday is the 17th. Big day. What are the plans for her birthday?"

He chuckled disbelievingly and stopped his pacing. "You know her. She wants to have Harper over. That's it. I mean, I guess they're going to get pizza or whatever. She doesn't want gifts. She just wants money. She said that even if she gave me a list, I'd probably get the wrong stuff, so it's just easier if I give her money and she gets what she wants. I can't pronounce half of what she's into. It all sounds Japanese."

"Well, I guess I don't feel bad about not being able to get over there," Ashley said.

Isaac snapped his fingers and then headed for the shelves in the far corner of the basement. "Carson and I will be back Friday morning for her birthday on Saturday," he said, while walking, "but I don't think we'll be a big part of the celebration." He pulled one and then another bag chair down from the topmost shelf. How many times had he shown up to a campground thinking he had everything only to end up sitting on stump because he'd forgotten a chair?

Too many times.

"Well, just have a good time with Carson. Sounds like he's receptive. Overall, it sounds like he's doing pretty good, right?"

Isaac set the bag chairs on top of the pile. He nodded. "Far as I can tell, he's good. Still doing the archery, humming along on his required hours for his driver's permit, and he doesn't burst into tears three or four times a day for no reason."

Ashley was quiet on her end. "Go easy. Having anxiety is no joke."

"I know. I know." He shook his head and then sighed breathily. "I guess it's like what we talked about last time." He set his free hand on top of the cooler and then lowered himself to sitting again. "What did you call it? 'Failure to launch'? Man, she's got that in spades. I don't know if she'll ever be an adult. She drives me crazy with the immature behavior. It's getting old. I think I'd need to put dynamite under her ass to ever launch her out of here. She just makes things so damn difficult that I—"

"I probably should get going, Dad. Ben's waiting for me so we can watch one of our shows. I promised I'd give him some time before I get too sleepy."

He nodded in agreement. He was making the conversation too negative. "Of course," he said. "I'll talk to you after the fishing trip."

They said their goodbyes.

Isaac sat for a moment on the cooler. That wasn't fair to do to her, he thought. She didn't need to hear so much venting. He made a mental note to try to stop unloading on Ashley like that. A feeling soon washed over him...a feeling that he wasn't alone in the basement. A presence was with him. Hairs prickling along the back of his neck, he shot up to standing and turned around.

Emily, wearing a t-shirt and pajama pants covered in cat silhouettes, stood on the bottom step of the basement stairs. With her eyes locked on him, tears streamed down her face.

Isaac swallowed. "Em—"

She turned and pounded up the stairs. "I'm sorry I'm such a disappointment to you," she managed through sobbing breaths.

Isaac covered his face with his hand. He drifted down to sitting on the cooler again. How much had she heard? Why had he even said it...about his own daughter? "Son of a bitch," he muttered into his palm. He looked up into the basement window. From the light of a nearby bare incandescent bulb, he could see the little moth suspended in a web, its body barely moving. Having come out of the shadows, a spider circled the insect, darting in and then back out, slowly paralyzing it with its venom.

CHAPTER 4

After years of living in the flat middle of the state, Isaac reluctantly pulled his attention from the rolling landscape beyond the highway's shoulder north of Gaylord. Something about this part of Michigan with its hills always made him think of Ireland. Or at least what he imagined Ireland to be. Up ahead, the exit sign for the village of Vanderbilt came into view. He smiled at the sight of it. In his late twenties and early thirties, he'd spent quite a bit of time fly fishing on the Pigeon and Black rivers, and Vanderbilt, as the signs in town indicated, was the gateway to the Pigeon River Forest.

"Here?" Carson asked.

"Yup," Isaac said. "Signal," he said. "And turn that down a bit."

"The exit is like a football field away." Despite his protest, Carson flipped his right turn signal on. Then, he turned the radio down to what amounted to muffled drums and bass guitar.

"It's the interstate," Isaac said. "People need more reaction time."

Carson eased the truck onto the exit ramp.

Isaac did some math in his head. It had been over twenty years since he had been in Pigeon River country. Before Ashley was born, he used to go two or three times a summer with an old high school buddy. They'd camp for a few days either on the Pigeon or on the Black River. He still remembered one of their best nights when they'd each landed a brown trout over fifteen inches. Walking back from the lucky bend in the river, they'd crossed a meadow lit by the full moon and shimmering with fireflies through the grasses. Then, celebratory beers around the campfire. It had been a damn near perfect night, like something out of a movie.

"What way?" Carson asked. He was idling at the stop sign at the end of the ramp.

Isaac told him to take a right and then directed him to the village market and gas station, one of the town's few thriving businesses. A few cars and a Jeep with a kayak strapped across its roll bars were parked at the convenience station.

"Pull up to the pumps," Isaac said. "Tank is on the right side. I want to gas it up before we head into the campsite."

Carson took a moment to process what Isaac had said. He then swung the truck around and eased the right side close to the pumps.

"Good job," Isaac said. "Smooth as silk." He opened his wallet, took out a credit card, and handed it to Carson. "Fill it up. I'm going to run inside and grab a couple New York strips for tonight. If you need to, get your phone stuff done because, like I said, we aren't going to have a signal once we get into the forest."

"Alright."

Isaac opened his door and took a slow jog toward the market. Breaking the news about no cell signal went better than he expected. Then again, he'd been breaking the news here and there with Carson over the past week. He took it much better than Emily would have. He couldn't imagine trying to camp with her. Food with a little ash from the campfire would be declared inedible. A small family of coyotes howling in the middle of the night would send her into hysterics. And God forbid she should get a wood tick embedded in her...a rarer occurrence in August, but still a possibility. He could almost hear her panicking as he imagined pinching the tiny body between thumb and finger and slowly backing its head out of her skin.

An old man stood at the entrance of the store holding the door open. Smiling, Isaac thanked him.

"You and your boy going camping in those woods?" he asked, nodding to the east.

Isaac gave the old man a onceover. A tattered baseball hat pressed his long, gray hair against the sides of his head. He wore a flannel shirt, old jeans with dirt stains packed into the knees, and rubber boots. Isaac looked into what seemed to be a kind face, eyes pale blue and inviting. "That's the plan," he said.

The old man shook his head. "I wouldn't. Bad weather coming."

Isaac was meticulous about checking the weather conditions before a trip. Every app, weather website, and television forecast contradicted the old man. Overcast skies with low eighties in the day and seventies most of the early night. A couple days of partly sunny. The chance of rain was negligible. Perfect for fishing. "Not according to my sources," Isaac said, smiling.

The old man waved his hand at him dismissively. "Machines and college degrees can't tell ya the weather. It's the bones that tell ya. I got an ache in my joints that says a big storm is coming. Wife's been getting migraines too."

"Hey," Isaac said, smiling, "talking like that, you're going to jinx it."

"Jinx got nothing to do with it. You get yourself some rain parkas. Storm's brewing."

Isaac nodded and started into the store. "I'll keep an eye out."

"Keep them both out." The old man grabbed his upper arm with a strength that Isaac wouldn't have guessed he had. "Things are afoot. Be careful in those woods."

Shaking off a chill, Isaac nodded. "Will do."

"You don't want to be soaked through. It's going to be a gully washer." The old man released his arm and shuffled away toward a compact pickup truck across the lot. Isaac imagined the rust-stained, single-wide trailer that the man was likely headed back to. He shook his head, letting the door shut between them.

Inside the store, he set steaks on the counter, and the cashier rang him up. He was tempted to grab a few other items, but he knew that he'd packed well and that they had plenty of food. A stack of pamphlets sat on the counter next to the register. The title read: *Discover the Wonders of the Pigeon River State Forest*. Isaac took one along with his receipt.

Exiting the store, he pulled his phone out. The still air smelled faintly of gasoline. He glanced toward his truck half expecting to see Carson on his phone getting last-minute business done while he still had service. Instead, he saw a girl about Carson's age with jet black, spikey hair and wearing a black t-shirt with pink piping on the sleeves and collar. She was standing at the driver's side window of the truck talking to Carson. Isaac shook his head and grinned. They hadn't even been in town for ten minutes. He had to admit, the kid had moves, though it did look like she was doing most of the talking. And smiling. Lots of smiling.

Isaac took a deep breath before dialing. He looked off toward the metal picnic pavilion that the town had put in adjacent to the rail trail. That and the dollar store were the only things new going on as far as he could tell. He hoped the Mill Street Diner was still open. He planned to take Carson there after they broke down camp on their last morning. The diner had good breakfasts. Damn near perfect hash browns as he remembered them.

Emily answered on her end.

"Hey," Isaac said. "I just wanted to let you know that we got to Vanderbilt. We're heading into the forest in a minute."

"So."

She clearly hadn't forgiven him for saying that she'd never grow up. But he knew it wasn't just that. She hadn't really heard it as him being concerned about her developing the skills to be an independent adult. What she heard was that he wanted her gone and that she was a burden and a disappointment. No matter how many times he tried to explain otherwise, she wasn't convinced. "I'd move out," she had said just the night before. "I would, but I don't know where I'd go. Harper's parents aren't exactly accepting of her sexuality, and I know they wouldn't want 'that skinny girl' living with them as a constant reminder. It's just we need a little starter money." He had told her that she didn't need to worry about moving out. At one point, he'd even listened to himself say that maybe Harper could move in with them. He'd been so wanting her forgiveness that he hadn't been sure what he was saying.

"So," he said, "I just wanted to let you know that we were going to lose cell service soon."

"Okay." A moment passed. "I'll try not to burst into tears."

She'd weaponized his own words. "Emily."

"What? You've gone over this with me a thousand times. You left me three different neighbors' phone numbers." She stopped and took a deep breath. "Having anxiety doesn't mean I can't function, and it certainly doesn't mean that you have to keep repeating things to me. I'm going to be fine. Just have fun fishing."

"Okay," he said. "Okay. I don't mean anything by this. I'm just letting you know that we will—"

"—drive into town on Thursday morning," Emily said in a tone that mimicked his voice, "and we'll call around noon just to make sure everything is good." Her tone changed back to her own. "I heard it the first five times you told me."

The girl that had been at Carson's window walked away toward a long sedan parked in the far corner of the lot under the shade of a tree. Moving languidly with a comfort beyond her years, she climbed in through the passenger door. Isaac couldn't make out the driver aside from the silhouette. Instead of being on his phone, Carson was looking over his shoulder towards the girl's car.

"Okay," Isaac said, chewing his lower lip. "I guess we're all set then."

"I guess so," Emily said. "See you when you get back."

"Okay, honey, see y—"

She'd hung up.

Isaac slipped his phone back into his pocket. He took a calming breath and started for the truck. Of course she was punishing him for what he'd said. It deserved punishment. What father talks that way about his own child, especially one struggling with her mental health? He pressed his fingertips back and forth across his forehead. But then, he had apologized, and she had said that she accepted. Doesn't that mean you move on? Even if he was in the wrong, she wasn't making it any better by acting immature and proving his point about her failure to grow up. He wasn't going to stand for being punished indefinitely.

He exhaled breathily and then opened the passenger door to the truck.

"Everything okay?" Carson asked. He looked at Isaac with some concern in his face.

"Hmm?" Isaac asked, climbing in and tossing the plastic grocery bag with the steaks between them on top of the console. "Oh, yeah, just going through in my head one more time to make sure we have everything. I think we're good." He buckled his seatbelt. Enough with Emily already. "And what about you, stud? Who was the girl you were talking to?"

Carson started the engine. "I don't know. She just came over to the truck out of nowhere and started talking to *me*."

Isaac looked over his shoulder toward the girl's car. It was gone. "What did she want?"

Carson shrugged. "She just asked if I was camping and said that she was camping with her older sister in a pop-up on Town Corner Lake. She said I should come over there if I wanted because they just sit around the campsite all day. They came into town because her sister wanted to text her boyfriend." Carson scratched his upper lip. "She said that she was kind of jealous that her sister had a boyfriend, but there aren't any guys at her school that she wants to date."

"What did *you* say?"

Carson shrugged again. "I don't know. I mainly just listened."

Man, she had really set Carson up. He was probably too inexperienced to take the bait. "Is that something you'd want to do? That campground they're in isn't far at all from where we're going to be. We'll have lots of downtime in the afternoons. I could drop you off over there for a couple hours at some point."

"I don't know. Maybe." He shifted into drive but kept his foot on the brake. "What way?"

Isaac told him he'd pull out taking a left and then take another left soon after onto Sturgeon Valley Road. "She looked cute," Isaac said as Carson pulled out.

"Dad."

"What? She did." He'd never really heard Carson talk much about girls. Maybe he wasn't all that interested yet. Or maybe like his sister, he wasn't interested at all.

Carson turned left onto Sturgeon Valley. "She was alright," he offered.

Isaac smiled. He'd bring up the girl again if they found themselves getting bored during one of their long afternoons. He'd let it lie until then. Looking out his window, he saw that not much had changed in what amounted to Vanderbilt's downtown. The tiny post office looked to still be in operation. The rest of the downtown was a collection of houses, some of which had been converted into businesses that had failed. A handful had boarded up windows.

They soon entered the Pigeon River Forest. Carson steered cautiously along the hilly curves of Sturgeon Valley Road. The road's surface was a mosaic of potholes filled with patching asphalt. Some potholes were slowly reforming, and he steered around the small craters. "We have about ten more miles," Isaac said. He opened the pamphlet in his lap and began to share with Carson the history of the forest. It was established in 1919, Isaac read, and it took visionaries to see the potential in the ravaged landscape. Between decades of logging and forest fires, what they originally started with could hardly be called a forest. "It's hard to believe," Isaac said, "but a lot of this was just stumps and burned over scrub land when they decided that they were going to reforest it."

Seeming to be listening, Carson glanced out the driver's side window now and again towards the trees.

Isaac continued to share from the informational literature. In the 1920s and 30s, they had made good progress with replanting trees, building fire breaks, and bringing elk back, not only into the forest, but into Michigan. On top of that, with grassroots encouragement, many people with private land in the area were deeding that property to the state. Isaac looked up from his reading. "Now that's generosity," he said. He knew that if he had land in the area, he would have held onto it. As it was, a few plots of private land, some with significant acreage, were dotted throughout the state property. In his younger days, he was often awestruck by the lucky few who had cabins right on the Black River.

Carson glanced into the trees again and then back to the road. "I read online that people have been seeing a huge wolf."

"What, here?" Isaac shook his head. "I don't think there are wolves in the Lower Peninsula."

"Well, people are seeing something," Carson said. "One guy said he and his wife and their baby were sleeping." Carson was talking fast. "It was hot in July, so he had his window flap open on the tent. He woke up because he had to pee, and the wolf's face was right in the window staring into the tent through the screen. The guy said it had eyes that practically glowed blue." Carson looked at his dad for a reaction and then back to the road. "Luckily he had a .357 and when he got it out and pointed it, the wolf took off."

"That sounds like a Second Amendment guy making up a 'good thing I had my gun' story."

"He's not the only one. Another guy said that he was hiking one of the trails, and he saw the wolf looking at him from over the top of trees that were like five feet high."

Isaac smiled sardonically. "That's a tall wolf, but more likely just a tall tale."

Carson looked out toward the trees again. "I don't think they can all be making it up. Like three or four different people saw something. Why would they all lie?" His voice sounded troubled.

"Oh," Isaac said, wanting to change the subject. He pointed to a sign that read *Song of the Morning Ranch*. "There's a yoga club down that road. They have a whole compound. Some pretty wild-looking buildings."

"Whatever. Is the campsite much farther?" Carson asked. He regripped his hands on the wheel.

"Not much. But when we come over that next rise, slow down and stop at the bridge you're going to see in a minute here. I want to take a look at the Pigeon."

After coming to it, Carson parked on the shoulder near the approach to the bridge like his father had instructed. They climbed down from the truck, walked, and then leaned on the bridge railing facing the upstream side of the river. The water flowed wide, flat, and lazily through the stretch. There was little shade or cover near the banks.

Isaac took a deep breath, feeling old feelings from the previous trips of his youth. He told Carson how he and his fishing partner had started every trip by walking up to the bridge to look at the river. "There's a campground right there," he said, pointing east beyond the bridge. He used his finger to slide his glasses back up into place on his nose.

Carson stared down at the flowing water. "Why aren't we just camping here then?"

"We're more likely to get into fish on the Black. Gotta fish the Pigeon more toward the night hours to get anything decent on. That's when the browns come out."

In the distance, Isaac heard the growl of a big diesel engine pulling a load up over a rise. He looked over his son's shoulder and then placed his hand on the teen's back and pressed him closer to the bridge railing. "Sit tight," he said.

Hazy in the distant heat rising from the asphalt, the front grill of a semi tractor came into view. It had to be going at least 50 miles an hour. Coming down the hill from the east, the logging truck stacked with timber soon barreled across the two-lane bridge like a moving wall. For a moment, the sound of it was the only thing that existed. Its passing trembled the tensile strength of the bridge up through their feet and into their legs. Isaac shook his head, watching the butt ends of the logs disappear around a corner. "That guy was going hell-bent for leather. He barely touched his brakes."

The last sounds of the truck doppled away in the western distance.

The back of Carson's hand tapped against Isaac's shoulder. "Dad, there's a guy standing in the water."

Isaac turned to look upstream. A man stood in the middle of the river just at a point before the view of the water disappeared around a bend to the east. His upper half was silhouetted in shadow, which only gave away the detail of his shaggy mop of hair. From his waist down, he wore jeans. No waders or hip boots as far as Isaac could tell. What the hell was this guy doing standing in the river fully clothed? His arms hung from his shoulders, and he seemed to be looking in the direction of the bridge. In his right hand he held what might have been a balled up, black garbage bag.

"He's not fishing," Carson said.

"Nope. I don't see a rod."

"What's he doing?"

Isaac shrugged. "Got me. Maybe river cleanup?"

The man took a step forward, adjusting himself against the current pushing him from behind. The bottom part of a gray sweatshirt came into view above his beltline.

Isaac took in a cold breath and then coughed it back out again. He shivered in what felt like a drop in the temperature. He shook his head slightly. Autumn was coming, no doubt about it, and the dragged-out months of winter would soon follow.

The man in the river steadied himself again awkwardly against the insistence of the current. Then he opened his fingers, and the black material fell out of his hand. It floated toward them on the current.

"What the fuck is he doing?"

"Carson!" Isaac stifled a grin.

"What? We're camping. We're men in the woods free from the rules of society."

It was a line Isaac had laid on him playfully the week before when he was talking up the trip. "Alright. Alright." He shook his head. "Smartass. Just go easy on the swearing...at least until you lose your first fish."

Carson sighed. "I'm going to look at the downstream side." He turned, looked both ways, and then crossed to the other side of the bridge.

When Isaac turned back from watching Carson cross, the man was gone. The only thing confirming that he had even been there was the small Rorschach of black floating slowly downstream toward the bridge. Isaac watched it as it took a more definitive shape, something like a black cross. It wasn't long before he realized that it was a dead raven with its wingspan spread out on the surface. It drifted toward him spinning in a slow circle. The head showed patches of bone where the flesh and feathers had rotted away. The eyes were long since gone from the sockets.

"River looks good over here," Carson called to his back.

Watching the raven approach, Isaac froze. His forehead beaded with sweat. What the hell was it with ravens? Why did he need to keep being reminded of that fateful card accident, the accident that had left him with a compromised leg...the accident that had taken his beloved wife.

Slowly waterlogging, the bird began to sink beneath the surface some 15 yards from its approach to the bridge.

A chill seized Isaac's body, the cold of it seeming to emanate from his bones. I'm not sure we should be here, he thought.

"Dad, you okay?" Carson asked, setting his hand on Isaac's shoulder.

Isaac turned and looked into his son's face. "What?"

"You were mumbling to yourself, and you don't look so hot."

Isaac turned back to the water and pointed at the black beneath the surface. "That's a little unsettling, wouldn't you say?"

"A garbage bag?"

"No, not a—" He took a closer look. Caught against some subsurface snag, a black garbage bag undulated beneath the current. Jesus Christ, he thought, I'm seeing things.

"That guy's gone."

Isaac nodded. "Yeah."

"I guess he decided river cleanup is some bullshit."

Isaac looked from the garbage bag to Carson's smirking face. "Alright there, Andrew Dice Clay."

"Who?"

"Never mind. Let's go. I want to get to the site and set up. We gotta stop at the DNR headquarters really quick too."

"Are you sure you're okay?"

"Yeah," he said. "I'm fine." He glanced one more time at the bag swaying in the current beneath the surface.

Goddamn ravens, he thought.

CHAPTER 5

The park headquarters, a gorgeous log cabin flanked by other log buildings and structures, was a mile or so down Twin Lakes Road. The inside walls were covered in pictures and displays of different flora and fauna that might be found throughout the forest. A stuffed bobcat looked ready to pounce from its birch branch high up on a wall. Taxidermized heads of deer and various pairs of antlers adorned the other walls. Carson stood gazing up at the height of a stuffed elk. Its massive rack of antlers stretched nearly three feet in width. The dark fur around its head segued into the tan color of its body and legs. Isaac smiled, seeing how clearly Carson was impressed by the enormity of the animal.

The ranger on duty, who'd identified himself as Dietrick Cross, returned from a side room and handed Isaac a campsite tag. He wore the standard khaki ranger shirt with slightly darker khaki pants. His prematurely gray hair, almost silver, was pulled back into a ponytail. His forearms protruding from his rolled sleeves were coated in thick hair. A shock of white chest hair poked out from his open collar. When taking the campsite tag, Isaac noticed the man's oddly long, squared off at the end, fingernails.

"You said, 'Isaac Fletcher'?"

Isaac tucked the campsite tag into his shirt pocket. He nodded, "Yes, sir."

Dietrick stroked his chin. "Your last name derives from a profession." He reached behind his neck and tightened the hair tie around the base of his ponytail. "Do you know what a fletcher does?"

"They make arrows," Carson said, turning his gaze from the elk.

The ranger swiveled his head towards him. "That's correct."

Carson had answered before Isaac could. With an eyebrow cocked, he looked at his son.

"What? I know things."

Isaac turned his attention back to the ranger. "I'm assuming you have a landline phone here."

He nodded. "Of course."

Isaac put his hands in his pockets but then pulled them out again and crossed his arms. "If I were to give my daughter...if someone called here and needed to reach..." It was asking too much. She'd be fine. She'd already made a big deal about how fine she would be. "You know what, forget it. Are we good to head to the campsite?"

Dietrick nodded. "You should be. Nobody has come in to get a tag for that site. That doesn't mean that it's unoccupied. Sometimes people will just go into that site, set up, and never get a tag."

Isaac shrugged a hand into the air. "I guess we'll take our chances. Worse comes to worst, we'll backtrack and stay at the Pigeon Bridge campground. It looked pretty empty when we came through that way."

"It sounds like you have a plan," the ranger said.

"We could stay at Town Corner Lake, too," Carson said. "You said that's not too far from the Black."

"And," Dietrick said, raising a finger. "Town Corner has vault toilets and a pump for water."

Isaac turned and offered his son a wry smile. "I don't think it's toilets or water access that's on his mind. He's got a lady friend camped over at Town Corner."

Carson turned his head back to the elk. "Oh, shut up, Dad."

Isaac laughed.

"Nothing wrong with keeping company with the fairer sex," Dietrick said.

Carson locked his attention on studying the elk's antlers, as though the two men had disappeared from the room. Isaac could see that the back of his neck was flushed red.

"Of course, you're not totally without facilities," Dietrick said, turning his attention to Isaac. "About 50 feet from where you'll be camped, someone made a makeshift outhouse. Even has a toilet seat. Of course, you're totally exposed, so don't let the Dogman catch you defecating out there. We've had a few alleged sightings this summer from hikers."

"What?" Carson asked from the other side of the elk. From the way he asked the question, it was clear that he hadn't quite heard everything.

Isaac snapped the ranger a fierce look that said, "Dude, come on, I'm trying to get the kid comfortable with the outdoors, not make him piss himself."

Dietrick seemed to understand Isaac's look. "Nothing, young man. Just telling your father that you do have a bathroom of sorts at the site but keep an eye out for hikers who might see you."

"The chances of someone coming by is slim to none," Isaac said.

Seemingly satisfied, Carson asked nothing else.

The Dogman of Michigan. Of course, Isaac had heard of the legend. Working with the Fish & Wildlife Service lamprey abatement department had seen Isaac camping for days at a time around the mouths of various Northern Lower Michigan rivers. That of course meant sitting around fires at night telling stories. He'd been on a team with a guy from Traverse City who was self-educated in Michigan legends and paranormal myths. He talked about the Paulding Lights, the Michigan Triangle, and Hell's Bridge over the Rogue River. He was especially obsessed with The Dogman. Half-man, half-dog, the seven-foot-tall Dogman presented as a werewolf of sorts. It was said to have a history all the way back to when Michigan was only inhabited by Native Americans. Early sightings included those by lumberjacks in the Nineteenth Century. Later, a man fishing on the Muskegon River claimed to be attacked by a pack of wild dogs, one of which stood on its hind legs. Numerous other sightings and encounters occurred throughout the 1950s and 60s.

Isaac believed in the Dogman about as much as he believed in Bigfoot, which wasn't much at all. But those stories didn't need to be in Carson's head, not when he's trying to sleep with nothing between him and the outdoors except for a thin wall of polyester. He already wasn't happy to find out that Isaac hadn't brought a gun.

Dietrick excused himself. Before leaving the room, he wished them an excellent stay in the forest. Isaac and Carson drove back down Twin Lakes Road, took a left on Sturgeon Valley Road and then a right on Tin Shanty Bridge Road. Soon they were on Chandler Dam Road whose curves followed the path of the Black River, out-of-sight through the trees to their right. Isaac looked behind them at the ribbon of dust they were raising from the dry dirt road. He didn't want it to come any time soon, but there was no doubt that they needed a good rain. They'd have to be extra careful with their fires. He hoped the river wouldn't be so low that it would drive the trout up into the colder water of the tributaries.

Along the way, Isaac had half-heartedly pointed out some various sights and turnouts, but more than anything, he focused on arriving and setting up. He wanted the work behind them and then a good evening on the river. He wanted the reprieve from the world that fishing often gave him. He longed for his focus to simply be likely good spots, rises on the surface, and watching his fly float through the bubble line off the end of a log. His mind lately had too often been on Emily. He still couldn't truly picture her doing anything beyond living in her childhood bedroom, playing house with Harper, and falling apart any time the world threw the slightest challenge her way.

As they turned through the final curve of Chandler Dam Road before their destination, Isaac spotted a car a hundred yards or so ahead of them pulling out onto the road. Its backend and taillights quickly disappeared into a cloud of dust as it raced away to the south. The car had come from the turnout that led down to the dispersed campsite.

Jesus, I hope they aren't camping down there, Isaac thought. He pointed Carson's attention to the right. "Turn here but go slow. There are some pretty big roots across the path. This is the two-track down to where we'll hopefully be camping."

"Hopefully?"

"Yeah, hopefully. Let's see if there's anyone set up down there. It can be a bit of a crapshoot getting this spot."

Carson guided them along the short path through the trees that opened out into a clearing with a rock-rimmed fire pit in the middle. Nobody was set up in the site. Isaac exhaled a held breath. He celebrated further yet when he noticed that someone had left seven or eight pieces of split hardwood.

Carson parked the truck in the long grass on the northeast side of the clearing where Isaac instructed. "We're parking here? I thought this is where we'd set up the tent," Carson said. "Less roots."

Isaac shook his head. "No, even this late into the season, you can still get wood ticks. That long switchgrass is the kind of terrain they love." Out of habit or tradition, Isaac reached down and patted the leather buck knife case attached to his belt. His father had given him the knife when he was a teenager. He always took it on camping trips.

For forty minutes, theirs became the language of setup, with Isaac giving instructions and both carrying out the tasks. Isaac had found a flat area among the roots on the south side of the clearing for the tent. The ground was mainly dirt with a loose layering of pine needles. Working wordlessly, they assembled their cots, rolled out sleeping bags, and set down their pillows. Outside of the tent, Isaac set a plastic tote for their shoes and clothes at the end of the night. If they did pick up any wood ticks during the day, they would go into the tote instead of coming into the tent with them.

The image of the dead raven surfaced from time to time in Isaac's mind. He shook it off. It wasn't a raven, he told himself. It was a garbage bag.

After slipping the steaks inside it, Isaac set the cooler in a spot that would have shade if the sun came out. He hoped to delay how quickly they would lose their ice to melting. He screwed the small canister of propane into place on the cookstove and checked the burners. With the touch of a match, both glowed with a circle of blue flame.

A chickadee landed on the branches of a wild cherry tree, pivoting its head and seemingly watching their progress.

Carson reached into the truck for the bag with the chips, cereal, cookies, and hotdog buns.

"Nope," Isaac said, "Just leave that bag in the truck. We'll use that as our pantry. We'll get critters sniffing around otherwise." He gestured toward a chipmunk scurrying around the edges of the campsite.

Isaac smiled and shook his head at the brief impulse to reach into the cooler for a beer to christen the campsite with that first sip. There was no beer in the cooler and, if there were, he wouldn't have touched it. Old habits die hard.

Before sitting, he went back to the truck and took out a plastic storage tote with a lid. Over the summer, he'd been cutting up some of the better-sized branches that fell in the yard. The night before their trip, he'd loaded the branches into the tote. He liked to arrive to a campground with at least a fire or two worth of dry firewood.

Carson set up his archery target, giving himself around a forty-foot challenge when the time came to shoot. Instead of taking his bow from the back of the truck, he took out his case and started assembling his fly rod.

Isaac looked up from setting the grill grate over the fire pit. "Itching to get out on the stream, eh?"

Carson shrugged. "Just want to be all set when we're ready to head out."

"Good thinking." Isaac slapped his hands together, knocking off grit and ash. He decided he could unpack the rest of the incidentals later. "I'll get ready too." He walked toward the back of the truck and grabbed his case. "What are you thinking of tying on?"

Carson threaded his leader and fly line up through the guides. "An Adams?"

Isaac nodded. "That's a good choice for most Michigan streams. I did stop at the fly shop in Midland. Guys there recommended we try a Purple Haze. I guess the brookies go crazy for them." Isaac flipped open his fly box and handed Carson a Purple Haze. "Try that. Switch to an Adams if you lose this in the tag alder."

With his young eyes and nimble fingers, he had the fly tied on in under a minute. He bit off the tag end of the knot.

"Nice work. You're getting good at tying those on."

Carson looked up at him. "Dad? I gotta go."

"Hmm?" Isaac then read the boy's face which said, "this isn't that hard to understand."

"Pretty much getting into emergency territory," Carson said. His forehead beaded with sweat.

They'd had fast food on the way up. Carson hardly ever ate it. He'd watched a documentary on the fast-food industry and swore it off ever since, aside from the occasional takeout pizza.

Isaac pointed to a trailhead that led to a path into the woods to the south. "I'd bet that leads to the toilet the ranger was talking about. Head down there. If you find nothing, take off your pants and underwear, grab a tree, and lean back like you're waterskiing. I'll bring toilet paper your way in a minute."

Carson stood up and bolted down the little path like something was chasing him. Isaac finished assembling his rod and tying on his own Purple Haze. Then, he took a roll of toilet paper from the pack they'd brought and walked it down the trail.

"Carson?"

Some twenty-five feet away he spotted him, fully dressed, zipping up his pants.

"What?" Carson said. "Don't look at me like that. I wiped. There was a roll of toilet paper in that can next to the toilet." The toilet was a two-foot by three-foot wooden box with a hole cut in the top. Someone had then used a tube or two of liquid nails to seal a toilet seat and lid over the hole. A rusty coffee can with a plastic lid held the swollen, slightly yellowed roll of toilet paper.

Isaac handed Carson a small bottle of hand sanitizer.

Carson squirted some into his palms and rubbed them together. His attention was locked farther down the trail. "What *is* that?"

Isaac followed his son's gaze. The overgrown footpath ran from the campsite past the makeshift toilet and further south to what Isaac guessed was access to the river. Not an official hiking trail, it had likely been blazed over the years by fishermen tramping it down into semi-permanence. The path stayed in their sightline until it took a sharp turn to the left. Something stuck out of the bend in the trail, resembling the handle of a lawnmower. Isaac shrugged. "Let's go check it out."

Carson walked a few steps behind Isaac. Soon they came upon a baby stroller parked in the middle of the trail. Isaac grabbed the handle and rolled it back and forth. "This thing's high end. I mean, not good for a trail like this, but Jesus...it practically looks brand new."

Carson walked past Isaac to the front end of the stroller. The long grass around it was bent and trampled. "Who would leave it here?"

"That's a good question. It doesn't really make any sense." Isaac pushed his glasses up the bridge of his nose.

He cupped his hand to his mouth. "Hello?! Anyone out here?" The birds in the trees around them went quiet. He waited a moment, listening. The birds started again. "Maybe somebody stole it and then decided otherwise... maybe got rid of the evidence?"

Carson crouched down and reached into the stroller's lower storage compartment. He pulled out two plastic snack bags. One held orange, fish-shaped crackers, and the other had little graham cracker bears. "That's weird."

Isaac took one of the bags from him. "This hasn't been out here long. Critters would have gotten into these."

Carson held up a stuffed elephant whose ears looked like they'd been used as teething rings. "Look at this."

Isaac looked at the toy. Then, he looked around them again. "Did we miss the Rapture or something?"

Carson tossed the elephant back into the stroller. "What if some stressed-out single mom came out here and drown her kid?"

"What?" Isaac looked at his son. "Jesus, Carson. That's pretty dark."

"Well, what do you think happened? It feels like something bad happened."

Isaac looked down the trail back toward the campsite. They'd wasted enough time with the stroller. Carson was starting to get fixated. If he turned it into one of his personal missions, they'd never get out on the river.

Isaac held his hand out and beckoned with his fingers. Carson handed over the other snack bag. Opening the zip seal on both, Isaac threw them farther into the woods away from the campsite. "I have no idea what happened here," he said, "but I know we have fishing to do."

Carson looked at him incredulously. "Aren't we going to go tell the ranger?"

Isaac laughed. "Tell him what? There's nothing to tell." He smiled reassuringly. "Look, probably some young parents came out here. They decided to walk their baby down to the river and dip its toes in the water. The stroller was giving them too much trouble on the trail, so they left it and carried the kid down there. They'll be back. Hell, we might see them while we're out fishing." He started walking the trail toward the campsite.

"Dad..."

He turned around. Carson was still standing next to the stroller. Isaac threw his hands up into the air. "Let's just fish, okay? When we get back, if the stroller is still here, we'll go up to the ranger station with it. Maybe they have a lost and found. I'm not doing that right now, though. This weather is too perfect, and we came here to fish."

Carson looked at him for a moment with his lips twisted off to the side. Then his mouth relaxed. He exhaled. "Alright. It just feels like this isn't good."

Isaac could feel that he needed to change the mood. "Hell, if the stroller *is* still here, maybe we'll swing through the Town Corner Lake campground on the way to the ranger headquarters. We can see what that girlfriend of yours is up to."

"Shut up."

When Carson caught up to him on the trail, Isaac tossed an arm around his shoulder. "Come on, lover boy, there's some big brookies out there with our names on them." Even with his jocularity, Isaac could feel that he was trying too hard... could feel himself trying to shake off the melancholy of the abandoned stroller.

CHAPTER 6

Isaac slipped his vest on and reached back to check that he could get his grip around the handle of his net. It hung from the back of his vest off a magnet release. He scanned their camping setup to make sure they hadn't left anything out, especially the cookies Carson had opened. He nodded his head at the cleanliness of their site.

Carson picked up his rod from where it leaned against a big pine tree.

"Ready?" Isaac asked.

Carson nodded.

"Shit, wait a second." Isaac crouched down and retied the lace on his left boot.

A crow cawed from a branch above them. Isaac stood and looked up in the trees. The bird perched on a branch some thirty feet above them, shifting its weight to one foot and then back to the other.

Isaac went cold, remembering the accident from over a decade ago. Gwen's bloodied face against the dashboard... Jesus Christ, it was like the memory was on a constant loop.

"You okay, Dad?"

Isaac shook off a chill. "Yeah, it's just a crow. We're good. Nothing here for him to scavenge, anyway."

Carson set his hand on Isaac's shoulder and gave it a gentle squeeze. Isaac's upper lip buckled in against his teeth when he looked into his son's empathetic eyes.

Isaac nodded. "Let's go catch some dinner," he said. He sniffed in a breath and then started for the trailhead that would lead them west to the river. He adjusted his glasses. Thinking of Gwen and everything they never got to do could still break his heart.

Carson followed Isaac through a tunnel of overhanging silver maple, cottonwood, and quaking aspen branches. The air was thick and humid in the marsh. The trail was a mix of higher dry spots and low swampy spots that tried, as they stepped, to suck the boots from their feet.

"This is the right way?"

Isaac didn't look back. A branch had already tried to rip the glasses from his face. "Just a little farther."

The swampy path opened out onto the river. Isaac stepped into it, and Carson followed him. The river was shallow at this spot and some twenty-five feet across. Downstream it flowed through a corridor of tag alder and then went out of site to the west. Isaac pointed upstream to where the main current doglegged around an island of grasses.

"This isn't like the Au Sable. Pretty hard to fish together. You should head upstream. Some good holes up that way." Isaac adjusted his glasses again on his sweaty nose.

"Why do I have to go upstream?"

Isaac reached down his waders into his pants pocket. "Because you're younger. I don't have it in me to work against the current like that. Plus, downstream gets pretty tight through the woods and then through a long stretch where you're flanked by tag alder the whole way. More likely you'd be snagging branches and snapping off flies." He finished pulling an orange strip of nylon from his pocket. He tied it around a branch right where they got in. "Upstream is pretty open for a few hundred yards. Good for casting."

Carson took his baseball hat off and dragged a sleeve across his forehead. "I stink at fishing upstream."

Isaac waved a hand at him. "Then practice. Or just wade upstream as far as you want and then turn around and fish it back. When you come around that little island, just keep your eyes on the left bank and look for this marker." He pointed to the hunter's orange ribbon that he'd just tied around a branch hanging above the water. Then he took his phone from his wader's waterproof pocket, looked at it, and then slipped it back. "It's almost seven o'clock right now. Let's meet back at the campsite at nine. You can come in earlier, but don't stay out later. I don't need to be worrying about you."

"What if I get into fish?"

"Just be back to the campsite at nine."

"Fine." Carson started toward the west side of the little island that split the current to either side of it. The way he trudged forward, it didn't look like he intended to fish until after he put the island behind him.

"Good luck!" Isaac called after him.

Turning to the downstream, Isaac pulled some line through the guides and then cast it back and forth a few times before landing the fly on the surface. With it being open and shallow, he didn't expect much from this stretch. He continued to work downstream, and as he moved closer to the first bend, he landed and released a few brookies in the five to six-inch range.

The bend took a sharp, nearly ninety-degree turn to his right. A fallen tree comprised nearly the entirety of the bend's left bank. The submerged underside of the tree offered perfect cover for trout. He took in a deep breath and exhaled it slowly. Being out on the river was working on him the way a thumb and fingernail could slowly pull and loosen a knot out of a shoelace. He was loosening and, for the moment, forgetting the frustrations of home. It wasn't without guilt that he realized that he hadn't thought of Emily once since stepping into the water. He listened to the birds in the woods, both near and distant, calling to each other. The air blowing out of the forest on a slight breeze had an earthy aroma.

And then there was the river...the constant shish and shimmy of it over its course. He'd taken Gwen fly fishing during the second summer they were together. She didn't bring a rod, but she did wear waders and walked along with him while he fished. After an hour, they found a small clearing in a grove of trees. They'd slipped into the grove and then slipped out of their clothes. Gwen had laid with her head on his chest afterwards, listening to the current, and she called the sound of it "murmuring." He liked that.

He closed his eyes for a moment and thought of the life in those depths in the darkness beneath the underside of the tree. How many fish were there? How big was the biggest? Did it hold against the bottom, ignoring what drifted by the log's edge that separated light from shadow? Did it wait instead for evening with the changes of light and cooler water temperatures? What were the factors involved that either brought a fish to the surface or kept it in the safety of the shadows?

It was largely a mystery.

Isaac opened his eyes and cast. The fly touched down within inches of the log. The current moved it even closer until it bobbed directly along the edge of the timber. Just as the line was going to run out of slack and he'd need to pull it back in, the Purple Haze disappeared off the surface. Isaac lifted his rod, guessing that a little whirlpool had sucked the fly under, given the laziness with which it had slipped from sight.

Instantly, the tip of his rod bent over with the pulling weight of a big fish. His heart jumped. He cranked in his slack line until he was playing the fish on the reel. It swam deep and hard for what Isaac guessed was the carved-out space under the log. With its upstream trajectory, it had the end of his rod bent into an almost perfect horseshoe.

"Come on. Come on," he muttered in something close to prayer.

He put steady pressure into the rod, trying to pull the fish out toward the middle of the current. He guessed the bank under the log was a tangle of branches and roots, all snags the fish could use to wrench the fly from its mouth.

Isaac kept up his pressure moving the fish slowly away from the underside of the log. The fish kept up its pressure toward the bank. The tension in the rod was getting to be too much. He'd hoped for the fish's exhaustion...that it would turn and head downstream. Instead, it gave everything it had and continued to make progress toward the bank under the log. As much as he wanted to land it, Isaac wasn't surprised at the moment of loss, when the hook let loose from the lip, and his line went limp.

The fish was gone.

Isaac stood silently in the river, his heart pounding like something trying to escape the cage of his ribs. The water continued around his legs, and the slightly metallic aftertaste of adrenaline watered into his mouth. He shook his head and resignedly wound in his line. "Goddamnit," he said under his breath.

Rounding the bend beyond the broken crown of the fallen tree, he looked downstream. The river's banks transitioned here from tag alder, water plantains, cut grass and duckweed to dry forest floor with a mix of hardwoods and pines. Branches jutted overhead, a constant hazard for snags and hangups while casting. I gotta keep my head in the game, he thought.

He stood for a moment reading the river. The next best spot looked to be a boulder near the water's edge. The current riffled over the riverbed upstream of the stone and then flattened over the depths surrounding it. A bubble line trailed off the far side of the stone.

A faint chime sounded from Isaac's waders. A rogue cell signal? He exhumed his phone from the waterproof pocket. He brought it out slowly, careful not to fumble it into the water.

He swallowed a rising of stress when he saw Emily's name. Her message was short and without context: *I asked for more hours at work.*

What did she mean this to be for him? Was it her saying, "Look, I'm taking your concerns seriously." Or was it more likely passive-aggressive bullshit? Her goal seemed to be for him to feel guilty: "Enjoy your fishing while I'm down here scrambling to build up some money before you throw me out on the street." Cryptic text messages from his children were among his least favorite. Ashley used to text him simply with the word *Dad* or *Dad?* When he would reply with *What?* the news that would follow was almost always bad: *My engine light came on* or *I have strep throat* or *financial aid reduced my amount.*

He glanced at the bars on his phone. Where they should have been were instead the letters SOS. Isaac stared at the letters. His mind started playing a small movie of him leaving the river, getting in the car, driving into Vanderbilt, calling Emi—

What was he doing? She hadn't texted about a housefire or to say that some burglar had tried to break in. She asked for more hours at work. Big deal. If he wanted, he could ask her more about it when they drove into Vanderbilt on Thursday. Enough of this. He went into his settings and turned his phone on airplane mode. He could spare his battery and keep anymore fugitive texts from getting through.

Just fish, he thought.

Casting to it, he had no strikes from the upstream side of the rock. He turned his attention to the downstream side.

When he cast, the fly bounced off the left side of the rock and then drifted downstream directly into the foam of the bubble line. His hands were tense and, rewarding his anticipation, a trout came up and sucked his fly off the surface. He lifted the tip, and the rod bent over with the weight of the fish. Instead of breaking for the root-tangled banks, it shot downstream, staying in open water. Yes, Isaac thought. The fish pulled line from the reel's arbor for twenty yards before Isaac could stop its trajectory and start to crank it towards him with a few turns of the handle.

"Isaac."

His body seized. Instantly he was as still as the boulder, and the river slipped around and between his legs. He was vaguely aware of the fish thrashing at the end of his line. A slight breeze rustled through the leaves.

His brother, Adam. His dead brother was speaking to him. He slowly turned his head, scanning both banks, unbelievably expecting to see his brother standing at the water's edge, a mop of curly hair, a crooked smile...

Nothing.

In his heart, he had known. It was the auditory tricks of the river. Water moving over stone and slipping its channels could create what sounded like voices on the wind. Still, the clearness of his brother's voice left him unmoving. It didn't sound something like his brother or almost imitate his brother. It was his brother, as though he were there fishing at his side.

Isaac's slack fly line snaked back and forth on the surface. He had unknowingly released the tension on his end of the fight. The fish had taken advantage and was long gone, nursing its lip somewhere under the surface. He couldn't bring himself to care that he'd lost it. It was one thing to hear voices on the river. It had happened to him many times before. It was another thing, a cruelty in its way, to so clearly hear his deceased brother.

He wound in his line slowly, trying to scan the water ahead for promising spots...trying to bring himself back to the fishing. He tapped the knuckle of his index finger against his forehead. Come on, man, just focus.

His brother's voice calling his name echoed in his head. What had Ashley called it when talking about the veterans that she'd spoken with during her internship?

Auditory hallucination.

The veterans would hear the voices of soldiers with whom they'd served. Sometimes voices from enemy soldiers they'd killed. Other times it would be the voices of their commanding officers or even just unknown voices commanding them to carry out self-harm. Therapists within the V.A. worked with them to keep them from dissociating.

Isaac had always listened intently whenever Ashley had spoken about her internship and her work with veterans. His father had done a tour in Vietnam and, though he rarely talked about it, the experience had left its mark on the man. Instead of going to any kind of therapy, his father had self-soothed his internal wounds with liquor. Maybe he'd have coped better if he'd tried talking to someone.

It was something Isaac knew he needed to think about for himself too. He'd never really spoken with anyone about his grief, at least not a professional. Only he knew how Adam had truly died. Only he carried the guilt of knowing that his brother was dead because of him.

He took in a long breath and exhaled. If I'd never invited Adam to the cabin, he would still—Stop. Just stop. He ground his lower lip between his teeth. A little harder and he would have drawn blood.

The river ahead flowed into a sharp bend turning toward the east. Water rushing into that corner had hollowed out a hole under the bank. Casting upstream of it and getting a good drift across its surface, he was certain that he could get another big fish to come up.

"Isaac."

He froze with his fly rod pointing straight up like the idle needle of a metronome. This time, his brother's voice sounded as though it had come from downstream. Isaac inhaled a chilled breath, like the first breath of stepping outside on an early winter morning.

Shaking his head, he cast to the bend, ignoring the chill creeping up his spine. His fly landed too far out from the bank. He let it drift, but no fish risked the two feet of open water to come out after it. He retrieved his line.

"Isaac?"

His brother's voice was mournful and held in its tone the question, "Why are you ignoring me?" Isaac turned nearly 360 degrees, scanning the woods. He felt idiotic at his impulse to say something, but there was nobody in the woods to hear him if he were making a fool of himself. He cleared his throat. "Adam?" He waited nearly 20 seconds for a reply. "Is somebody talking to me?" Listening, he heard nothing save for the song of the current. He took a few deep breaths. His heart slowly calmed. A tear slid down his cheek, and he brushed it away.

After a moment, he cast to the hole again, but in his haste overshot and snagged on a skinny root protruding from the bank. He watched the end of his leader, and the fly knotted to it, turn several loops around the twisted finger of wood. Goddamnit, he thought. There would be no pulling that snag free, short of snapping the fly off and tying on another. The hole was promising, but not that promising. He would need to wade right into it to retrieve the fly, which would scatter any fish.

With his rod pinched between his arm and ribs, he fumbled the fly with his fingers, slowly untwisting it from the root. Sweat beaded across his forehead. He swiped at mosquitos buzzing his ears and gnats flitting in front of his face. His eyes weren't what they once were, and even with his glasses he had trouble seeing how many times the thin leader was turned around the root. After a minute, he finally had the fly free.

"Isaac!"

He bolted up straight like his spine had been replaced with a length of rebar. He'd heard that desperation in his brother's voice before. They were much younger, Isaac 15 and Adam 7. They were at their father's deer camp in the early summer. Isaac had headed out across the meadow to check on his deer blind after what had been a punishing winter of heavy snows. He half expected that its roof might have caved in. Adam had trailed behind him, pleading for him to slow down. Isaac ignored him. Then the scream had come, different from the consistent whining and spiked with panic. When Isaac had turned to look, his mind put the details together quickly. Trying to keep up, not watching his footing, Adam had tripped and landed right in a sand hornet's nest. Even decades later, Isaac could still picture him flailing on the ground under a small haze of air freckled with angry hornets. He screamed Isaac's name over and over. Isaac had run back to him, dragging him from the nest while getting stung a dozen times himself.

Their father had raced them both into the hospital in Gladstone where Adam was treated and kept overnight for nearly 100 stings.

Isaac had always blamed himself.

Heart racing, he looked downstream in the direction the shout had come from. Some fifty yards from him, the river turned sharply to the south. In the bend, the upper half of a man jutted up from the water, his legs beneath the surface. His right hand was wrapped around the trunk of a young cedar. He was pulling himself up from the water onto the bank.

The mop of curly hair. The ever-present college sweatshirt.

"Adam!" Isaac shouted.

The man lost grip of the branch and slid back down into the water. He turned abruptly and faced Isaac, wide-eyed. With a beard and straight, ginger hair coming out from the sides of his hat, he looked to be in his early forties. He certainly wasn't Adam.

"What?! Holy shit, man. What the hell!" He stood with his fingers splayed over his chest holding himself steady in the deeper water of the bend.

Isaac launched an extended palm as apology. "I'm sorry. Jesus. I thought you were someone else. I didn't—"

"Christ," the man shouted. His cheeks puffed out and then he exhaled. "Give a guy a goddamn heart attack, why don't you?"

Isaac pulled his glasses off and massaged his other hand over his face. "I really am sorry! I thought—"

Shaking his head, the other man turned back to the business of pulling himself from the water. Seemingly charged with adrenaline, he made short work of the task and was soon standing on the bank. He bent over, retrieved his fly rod from the ground, and then stalked off into the trees. "Fucking idiot," he shouted without turning back to look at Isaac.

Isaac watched him until he was absorbed into the woods. The settling of his own adrenaline left him feeling sick. He stood with his hand on his forehead staring up into the overcast sky. "Jesus Christ, little brother, what's going on with me here?"

He scanned the river ahead and spotted a downed tree near the bank. He made his way to it and sat. The thought came to him that they could just bag the rest of the trip. The dead raven floating down the river. Disembodied voices. His mind clearly wasn't in the best place. Going back home, he could check in with Emily and see what her text was all about. Maybe he could finally sit down with her, and they could try again to understand each other. He would talk to her outright, "Hun, I'm out of my depth here. That's on me. But maybe you could just tell me what you need from me." The idea of packing and leaving the next day flooded him with relief. As he pictured them on the highway headed back south, dread wicked up out of him and rose away like mist coming off the river in the morning. Carson probably wouldn't care. If he was upstream getting skunked, he'd come back to camp disappointed and doubtful of the rest of the trip. If that were the case, he'd be more than willing to leave with the sunrise.

Sitting, sifting through his thoughts, Isaac began to shake his head. Christ, I'm sitting here hoping the kid doesn't catch any fish. What was with all the planning if we're just going to head home after one day? He'd wanted to instill a love of the outdoors into his son, the same way his father's deer camp had done for him.

He stood up. Blowing air over his Purple Haze, he then dosed it with floatant. He flicked a few short casts downstream to draw out more line. Then, he began toward the next bend where the other fisherman had just gotten out. That was one of the lessons a river taught. A river was like life, and each downstream bend came with the promise of opportunity. One just needed to keep moving forward.

We're not going anywhere, he thought. I'm going to see this thing through.

CHAPTER 7

The sun had set in the western sky. Twilight was moving toward dusk. Isaac circled the big, gnarly pine standing watch over the campsite. Finding where some past fisherman had pounded a nail into the tree, he hung up his waders. Carson's were already hanging a few inches away with his fly rod leaning against the bark nearby. They'd both arrived back to the site at nearly the same time. Carson had just moments before peeled off his waders, hung them, and slipped on sneakers before jogging down the trail in the direction of the toilet.

"Round two with the fast food?" Isaac called after him. He received no reply. He smirked.

Isaac slipped on his untied hiking boots and walked over to the cooler. Opening it, he looked down at two brook trout, each in a sealable sandwich bag. Carson had caught a ten-incher not long after turning the corner of the upstream island. The sun had been backlighting the treetops in the western distance when Isaac's nearly 11-inch fish had come out of the shadows of a tag alder just downstream from where the other fisherman he'd startled had climbed out of the river. Their once bright fisheyes were already glazed over with a glaucoma-like haze. The vivid hues of their bodies from when they were first in hand had dulled like a watercolor painting brush stroked in fugitive pigments, making them look drained of spirit.

Something about the melancholy of seeing the fish like this made Isaac wish he could be a catch-and-release guy. Why the need to kill them, to possess them in the most permanent sense? Why not let them live? Then again, he'd heard theories, even from biologists in the Fish and Wildlife Service, that catch-and-release was just a placebo for bleeding heart types. After the surprise of getting hooked and the struggle of the fight, especially prolonged fights, the fish's system went into shock. They swam off, sure, but never fully recovered from the adrenaline jolt, eventually suffocating and then turning belly up. That was one theory anyway.

Isaac closed the lid to the cooler.

"It's gone."

Isaac turned. Carson's silhouette was just coming from the latrine trail. "What?"

Carson pointed behind him toward the darkening woods. "The baby stroller. Somebody got it."

"I told you they would," Isaac said, nodding. He'd forgotten about it.

"I feel bad now that we threw the snacks away."

Isaac chuckled. "Well, don't. We probably saved them from coming back to a stroller full of squirrels." He opened the cooler again and dug down until he came out with the grocery bag holding the steaks. "I'm going to get these ready. Gather up some kindling and get a fire started. There's newspaper in the utility box."

"What box?"

Isaac pointed at it next to the table he'd set the camp stove on. "That one."

"Didn't you already bring wood?"

Isaac walked the steaks over to the little table. "I didn't bring kindling. And, you'd better gather some up soon. You're losing light. Unless you want to eat raw steak and fish."

"Did we bring the stove for decoration?"

Isaac shook his head, grinning. "Just get the kindling, smartass."

Both bent to their work. Carson gathered up sticks and had a fire going just as the evening had gathered in the darkness around them. Isaac salted the steaks and smeared butter inside the cavities of the gutted fish. Afterwards, he wrapped the fish and two more slabs of butter in tinfoil. While he waited for the fire to burn down, he opened a can of sweet corn. Then, remembering them, he went to the tent and dug through his duffel bag. He found the edibles he'd picked up at the dispensary to help him sleep. Ashley had told him to make sure he took it before he ate. "Following it with a meal helps it metabolize in your system. If you eat the meal first, it can slow down the process," she'd explained. He studied the edible in his palm. "Body of Christ," he said smiling and then popped it in his mouth. Unlike the Eucharist of his youth, Isaac chewed the edible. Nodding his head, he agreed that grape razzle was a good description. A slight flavor of weed came through in the aftertaste.

When the higher flames of the fire were down, he layered the bed of coals with a carpet of kindling before setting the grill grate over the fire pit. He set the tinfoil on one side of the grill and the steaks on the other. The kindling flared up but quickly burned down and then added to the glowing bed of embers. Using pliers, he set the can of corn in the coals.

Carson sat in his chair watching.

They soon ate from paper plates with plastic utensils. Isaac added a few thicker branches to the coals and then let the fire that followed burn the fat and gristle from the grill. Emptying its contents onto their plates, Isaac tossed the corn can back into the coals. The last of the water inside of it sizzled while the outside blackened and charred. The steaks and fish had turned out near perfect. "Nothing like fresh trout over a fire," Isaac said. Carson hummed a noise of agreement in his throat. When they were finished eating, everything went into the fire. Their plates and utensils. The plastic and foam backing that had packaged the steaks. Even the tin foil the fish had been cooked in. He added a few more logs once all their garbage was in the fire pit.

"I don't think that's exactly environmentally friendly." Carson crossed his arms and leaned back in his seat.

"I know. But if we don't do it this way, we'll have raccoons coming in to check out the smells all night. They can make a racket, too. We both need to get a good night's sleep if we're going to hit the river again in the a.m." Isaac settled himself into his chair.

For a time, they sat staring into the flames. Isaac found a branch on the ground that a previous camper had used as a fire poker. He used its burnt end to sift the trash in the fire, making certain all that could be burned was burned. The corn can and the tin foil were so blackened that there was no way they were giving off any odor of food.

They each took turns telling the tales of their fishing. Carson had the keeper early on, but afterwards he hadn't landed anything bigger than six inches. He said that just when it was getting to the point where it felt right for the surface to be freckled with feeding fish, instead it turned off completely. For the last half hour before he came into camp, he'd had zero strikes. Isaac told his own stories about fishing through the woods and then fishing under the tag alders farther downstream. He'd left out the parts about his brother and about startling the other fisherman.

A haze hovered at the edges of Isaac's vision. His ears rang with a steady tinnitus. He opened and closed his mouth a few times against the feeling that somehow his jaw was misaligned. Then he smiled to himself. It must have been the marijuana kicking in.

"Hey," he said, pivoting his gaze toward Carson, "did you hear anything out on the river?"

"What? Why do you sound like that?"

Isaac blinked. He looked across the flames and rising smoke of the fire. Carson sat mostly in silhouette with flashes from the fire intermittently illuminating parts of his face. The weed was getting into Isaac's voice, slightly raising the pitch. "I don't sound like anything. I'm just tired. It's been a long day."

"What would I have heard out on the river?"

"Nothing." How would he even begin to bring it up? "Hey, when I was out on the river, your dead uncle was trying to talk to me," he imagined himself saying. Not only did the story make him sound nuts, but it probably wasn't the best to share right before they try to go to bed in a pitch-black campsite in the middle of nowhere. Poor kid might have a hell of a time getting to sleep with that banging around in his head, not to mention those far-fetched wolf stories. "I just thought I heard a loon," Isaac said, attempting some misdirection. "I don't know if I've ever heard a loon out here. I mean, while fishing the Black. Have you heard a loon? I mean, did you hear a loon? Tonight, I mean."

Carson didn't say anything for a moment. "I think I'm listening to a loon right now."

Isaac laughed. "Yeah, I'm not making much sense." He laughed again and then yawned. "I'm getting punchy."

"Guess so." Carson cleared his throat. "Do you think tomorrow afternoon we could go over and check out the Town Corner campground?"

"Ooh, Town Corner, eh?"

"Dad."

"Alright, yeah, we can check it out after the morning fish." Isaac yawned again. "Man, I'm getting tired. Are you tired?" He felt that if he didn't get up soon, he might not get up at all.

"I could probably sleep. I brought ear plugs."

"Ear plugs?"

Carson stood up. "Yeah, for your snoring."

"Fair enough." Isaac looked at the fire. Flames were still dancing off one of the larger logs he'd tossed in. It would burn for at least another hour. "Fire is looking really pretty. Seems a shame to douse it." When he stood up, the world tilted under his feet. "Oh boy."

Carson stood next to the tent undressing and putting his clothes in the plastic tote. "What?"

Isaac blinked. "What?"

Standing in his underwear, Carson bent over and unzipped the door to the tent. "What do you mean, 'What?'... you just said, 'Oh, boy.'"

"No, I didn't."

Carson stepped inside the tent. "Anyway, goodnight, Dad. Get some sleep. I think you need it."

"Okay. Night." Isaac stepped away from the halo of light around the fire pit. Carson shished and shimmied his way into his sleeping bag. Isaac smiled at the slippery sound of it. It was a sound he hadn't given much attention in the past, but he liked it. The darkness loomed the farther he got from the fire, made darker still by all the trees circled around their campsite. Isaac unzipped and started taking a leak. Up above, stars freckled the sky. No cloud cover to speak of. "Sweep in sle... sleep in sweats if you packed them. It could get cold later."

Carson didn't respond. Probably had his ear plugs in already. Gas trapped in the pores of the flaming log popped, sending tiny embers that winked out in the dirt just outside the fire pit ring. A ground-level breeze slinking out of the marsh-moist landscape around them chilled Isaac's ankles. A branch snapped in the wooded darkness. Listening, he shook himself. Another branch snapped. Something was making a slow, curious approach toward the campsite. He guessed it was a deer. A coyote would be unlikely. Whatever it was it had some weight to it. "Get," he said sternly. He zipped his pants. The snapping branches in the woods went quiet. He imagined that through the night, dozens of animals would approach the periphery of their campsite. Some would linger on the edges. Others would come all the way in to see what scraps of food might be found.

Isaac staggered. The ground felt as though he were walking on a funhouse's tilted floor. When he made it to the tent, he undressed and then deposited his clothes in the same tote Carson had used. His fingers fumbled on the tent's zipper and, after his third failed attempt at grabbing it, he started laughing. In a cacophony of plastic zipper teeth, polyester, and labored breathing, he finally unzipped the door and nearly fell inside. Not wanting to disturb Carson, he zipped the flap closed as quietly as he could. He held still and listened. Nothing, save for the sound of his son's low, steady breathing. Those had to be good ear plugs.

Stripped down to underwear, Isaac shivered. His teeth clicked together, and his skin pimpled with goosebumps. He sounded as though he had a stutter when he mumbled Christ's full name in vain under his breath. He rifled through his duffel bag. Pulling out sweatpants and a hoodie, he pulled them over his shaking body. He groped in the dark. Finding his sleeping bag on top of his cot, he wedged his legs and then torso inside. He didn't care about the pleasing sound of the sleeping bag material anymore. He just wanted to get warm. He pulled his knees up to his chest and lay in the fetal position, balling in around him what warmth he could find.

His shivering subsided after a few minutes. He could feel himself at the edge of sleep. The edible was helping. Fuzzy half-dreams drifted into consciousness and then back into half-dreams again. Warmed, he stretched his body out to its full length. He lay on his back. The half-dreams started again. He wasn't here. He wasn't anyone. He was floating. He smiled wistfully in the dark, finally seeing that life was a temporary lark. Clinging to some kind of safety, some kind of constant, was for fools. It was a recipe for misery, he realized. In a ship going down, you don't fret over the cleanliness of the linens. You enjoy the slow descent. Look out a port window. Revel in the view of the vast ocean.

Then a new thought washed in like a tidal wave. He was trapped. His arms were pinched against his side, his breaths shallow. He couldn't move. Panicked, he pulled his arms from inside the constricting sleeping bag. He took a deep breath. He felt better. If he was honest with himself, he'd always had a bit of claustrophobia. That's all it was...he had just needed to free himself from the sleeping bag's suffocating hold on his arms.

But he wasn't free. He could feel it coming for him from out there in the hazy future. Someday, he'd have to have an MRI. Everyone did eventually. It wasn't enough that the machine itself was scanning for every trace of tumor and disease. It was the process. Slid into a tube, like a corpse pushed back into its place in the morgue. Buried alive. The closed-in, suffocating feeling had him at the edges of panic. An urge to get out of the sleeping bag consumed him. Another part of him knew that the chattering cold was waiting for him if he did get up. His heart raced.

He lay with his arms pressed to his side. He could practice, he decided. The idea of an MRI was worse than the thing itself. Right? He closed his eyes. He imagined the curved plastic inches from his face. He took deep breaths and released them slowly. They let you listen to music. In some, you could turn your head and see outside. Even watch television. He'd heard that. He was certain of it. He could handle it. His eventual MRI would be no big deal if he approached it with the right mindset.

Soon, his breathing matched the sleeping rhythm of Carson's breaths. The half-dreams began again. I'm going to sleep, he thought. I'm going...

And then an image from Facebook crowded in. It was an illustration of a man who had gone caving. "Can you imagine?" someone had captioned in their reposting of the picture. Inching his way through a tight passage of rock underground, certain it had to lead somewhere, the caver had ended up instead stuck, upside down, in a constricting dead end. The illustration simply showed a cartoon silhouette of the man and how he had been positioned. Isaac could feel the jagged rocks pressing into his skin. The blood rushing to his head. Twenty-seven hours the man had been suspended there. And then he'd died. What madness had he experienced in those interminable hours? What unknown levels of panic had seized him? In time, his headlamp had flickered out. It was just him, wedged into the cold stone of the pitch-black passage. Isaac was there. He felt his own elbows jammed into his ribs. His hands were folded under him against his sternum. Struggling against the constriction only made it worse. He couldn't...

his ribs had no room to expand...he couldn't...he couldn't breathe...

Gasping, Isaac sat straight up. He was in a tent. He was camping. He nodded almost imperceptibly. Carson lay not far from him, snoring lightly. Isaac took a deep breath through his nose and exhaled through his mouth. He shook his head in the fuzzy darkness. An MRI? Caving? What the hell was his subconscious doing to him? He tried to lie back again. For a moment, he was good. He thought he might even drift off. Then, the claustrophobic anxiety returned and escalated with each passing minute. He leaned up on an elbow and, bending, retrieved his glasses from the tent floor alongside his cot. He bent again for his baseball cap. The stifling air in the enclosed space of the tent lacked oxygen. His tinnitus roared. A steady current of low-grade anxiety pinged between his shoulder blades. After a moment, out of instinct, he crawled across the floor of the tent and unzipped the door flap. The fresh night air rushing through the opening intoxicated him. He stayed on hands and knees for a moment, breathing it in. That's what I need, he thought. I need to calm down. I need to breathe. He stood up into the night and zipped the flap closed again.

A damp chill hung in the air. Isaac wasn't sure of the time. He guessed it was after midnight. Maybe he had slept some. The campground was lit in the soft blue light of the nearly full moon. Everything was still. It had to be late. Isaac grasped the back of his chair and then lowered himself into it. The fire was down to a bed of glowing coals giving off the faintest hiss. He closed his eyes.

In the darkness behind his eyelids, he searched for comfort. Thoughts instead wanted only to bring him concern. How long had it been since he'd had a checkup? When he turned 50, he went to the doctor for the first time in a decade. He was amazed they'd given him a clean bill of health. He made a vow. For several years in a row, he kept yearly appointments, kept his promise. Then, somehow, over the last few years, he'd gotten away from it. He felt fine, but that didn't matter. It was the bloodwork. He hadn't had a draw in over three years. You could feel fine, but the final analysis was in the bloodwork. It wasn't as though cancer wasn't in the family. With his mother's cancer, before anything else, they were tipped off by a high white blood cell count. He could have a tumor growing in him undetected. That odd pain on his left side...

He stood up and paced around the fire ring. It seemed the only thing to calm him, as though he, while moving, could stay one step ahead of his troubling thoughts.

In time, he sat in his chair again. If he were going to sleep, he would have to be able to be still. He couldn't pace and sleep. He was fine. Everything was going to be fine. He was just overly tired. And he was high. Too high. But in the morning...

He snapped his dozing head up from his chest.

Emily.

He was failing her. Was this what it was like for her to live with anxiety, where every thought felt like a weapon you were pulling on yourself? If he was honest, he usually met her anxious thoughts with irritation. Hadn't he dealt with enough? But if she felt like this, suffocating in anxiety, what solace was his anger? How could he have been so heartless?

There was something wrong. Something bad was going to happen with her. She shouldn't be here. He shook his head. What? he thought. *He* shouldn't be here. They shouldn't be here. They should pack up in the morning. He needed her to know that he knew—

A branch snapped in the woods near the tree line. Isaac lifted his drowsy head from his chest. He turned toward the sound and scanned the misty darkness. For a moment, he had difficulty swallowing. Something was there, some upright silhouette...a darker shadow in the blue-black darkness of the woods. Another footfall and then another. The outline of a man soon shambled toward him. Somewhere in the distance a family of coyotes took to howling.

Isaac gripped the arms of his chair. He could feel his pulse behind his ears. "Hey," he said, "you're walking right into a campsite here. Don't want to startle you." He'd only tried it a few times in his youth, and without any luck, but they said the biggest fish on a fly were sometimes to be had at one or two o'clock in the morning. This guy was probably a diehard fisherman coming off the water. "Any luck out there?" Isaac asked.

The man took a few more steps toward the fire pit. He carried nothing with him, wore no waders, and his arms hung at his sides. An odor of sulfur drifted in on the air.

Isaac wrinkled his nose. "Hey, you okay?"

The man took another step and moaned faintly in his throat. "I'm eyes..."

"What?" Isaac felt as though he were swallowing his heart back into place. That voice... it couldn't be. His hand, seemingly acting on its own, drifted up and fumbled along the bill of his cap. His fingers found the switch to his headlamp.

Light flashed. He squinted as his eyes adjusted. In front of him, in the hard beam of the headlamp, stood his dead brother. His mop of curly hair was twisted through with branches and leaves. His pale eyes stared out from the ashy skin of his face. He wore his Eastern Michigan University sweatshirt and jeans, soaked from the mid-thigh down. He had no shoes nor socks on his wide, gray feet. "Gone," he groaned. "I'm gone."

A tear broke from Isaac's eye. "Adam?"

"Dad?"

Isaac turned.

Carson stood in the sudden spotlight with his legs in the tent and his body upright outside of it. He held up his arm to shield his eyes from the hard light. "What are you doing? Turn that off."

Isaac reached up and touched the switch. Everything was instantly black. He blinked, waiting for his vision to adjust.

The darker silhouettes of the trees faded in to view. Isaac surveyed the space around him. Adam was gone, as though he'd never been there. Moving off as quickly as he had seemed to, he would have made some kind of noise, especially among the leaf litter and fallen branches in the woods. He couldn't have just disappeared.

It was a dream. He'd fallen asleep in his chair. Carson had woken him. That's all that happened. Isaac stood. His heart drubbed in his ribs as though someone were working it like a speedbag. Sweat cooled uncomfortably along the back of his neck.

"Dad? What the hell are you doing out here?"

Isaac looked at Carson. The teen was ghostly gray in the moonlight diffused through the trees. "What?"

"What are you doing out here?"

Isaac blinked. "I don't even know." In the moment, he knew only one thing, and that's that they were leaving the next day. They could get up in the morning and fish. They could hike one of the trails or go to an elk viewing area. Hell, they could even go into town and have a pizza from the diner. But they wouldn't be staying another night. He was too preoccupied with Emily. His subconscious was clearly too preoccupied with the guilt surrounding his brother's death. He was almost certain that he'd get no sleep if they stayed another night. Despite his exhaustion, he wasn't even sure that he'd be able to sleep when he followed Carson back into the tent.

"Dad?"

Isaac nodded. "Yeah, I'm coming. Sorry."

CHAPTER 8

Navigating the truck along the curves of Chandler Dam Road, Isaac yawned into the back of his hand. The skin around his dry, tired eyes pulled at the corners when he blinked. He studied the sky through the windshield. Another overcast day. The rearview mirror showed the dust storm they were raising behind them. Carson had the passenger side sun visor pulled down. He fussed with his hair in the little mirror. Then he reached up with both hands, making ready to squeeze a blemish on his cheek.

"Don't do that," Isaac said. "You'll make it worse." Carson looked at him, and Isaac slapped his knee affectionately. "You look fine. You can barely see it."

Carson took his hands from his face and flipped the sun visor back into place.

"She's camping too. It's not like she'll be all dolled up."

"Dad."

Isaac lifted his right hand from the steering wheel in a surrendering gesture. "Alright. Alright, I'll just drive." Dolled up? Jesus, he thought, I'm sounding like my father more and more every day. He yawned again, uncertain how much sleep he'd finally had the night before.

Ashley was often good with her advice, but this marijuana for insomnia experiment had been a bust. He planned to pitch the remaining edibles into the garbage. As he'd lain in the tent, he'd also promised himself that he would seek out a therapist. The circumstances around his brother's death, and the culpability Isaac felt from those circumstances...well, a better mind than his own would need to help him untangle and heal. Sure, he wouldn't be able to be completely truthful. Maybe it would be enough to say that he'd invited his brother to the island, and his brother had likely drowned. It was close enough to the truth that they could talk about his feelings of guilt.

Earlier that morning, he and Carson had crawled out of the tent. The level of light in the eastern sky, even through cloud cover, indicated to Isaac that they'd overslept. By the time they'd geared up and headed for the river, it was nearly eleven a.m. They fished together in the wider stretch upstream of the little island. Neither of them had many strikes nor landed fish. They were off the river again before half past noon.

A porcupine waddled down the right side of the road in front of the truck, interrupting Isaac's recollection of the morning. He slowed, giving it space in front of him, until the porcupine turned up the sandy shoulder and into the woods.

"I betcha he's a bit of prick," Isaac said.

Carson looked at him. "Really?"

"Man," Isaac said, grinning, "tough audience." He pressed the gas.

Back from fishing that morning, he had used the cookstove to make them a brunch of scrambled eggs, bacon, hashbrowns and toast. While his father cooked, Carson used the time to practice with his bow. His groupings of six arrows were consistently within an inch of each other with the occasional two-inch outlier.

While they were eating, Isaac had brought up the idea of packing and leaving sometime before dusk. He hadn't been sure how Carson would react, but was relieved enough when he shrugged and said, "Sure. I don't care."

After they'd eaten and cleaned up, the notion to head over to Town Corner Lake campground surfaced suddenly in Isaac's mind, like a trout coming up from an unlikely spot on the river. Though responding nonchalant, Carson's immediate fussing with his hair and clothes had betrayed his excitement at the prospect of seeing his mystery girl. He asked to borrow Isaac's comb. After noticing some scrambled eggs dry-crusted on it, he'd even changed his shirt. It wasn't long after that they'd hopped in the truck for Carson's rendezvous.

Driving north on Blue Lakes Club Road, Isaac soon turned right onto the two-track that would take them to where the girls were camping. Flat and glassy, Town Corner Lake itself flashed into view through the mainly coniferous trees outside of Carson's window. A faint piney smell filled the truck's cab. A dozen campsites were located on the northeastern side of the small body of water. None of the sites were occupied save for one with a pop-up camper and the sedan they'd seen the girl get into at the Vanderbilt market. The girl herself reclined in a zero-gravity chair under the shade of a Scots pine. She looked to be reading a book. Her view was picturesque overlooking the entirety of the little lake.

"Looks like they're home," Isaac said, smiling.

"Maybe just turn around," Carson said. He studied her shyly through the windshield.

If she heard the truck coming, she hadn't looked in their direction yet. "You'd be disappointed later if we don't stop and say hi," Isaac said.

"Just drive past."

The door to the pop-up opened, and the older sister stepped down to the green turf rug they had under their canopy. She wore no shoes, black sweatpants and a dark gray hoodie with the hood up over her head. Her black hair jutted out from the edges of the hood and framed her face. She held a red-flecked-with-white metal coffee cup. A straw and a leafy-tipped rib of what looked to be celery stuck up from the beverage. She glanced toward the truck, pointed, and then her mouth moved. The younger sister swung the front of her chair down. She gazed over her shoulder toward the truck, smiling and waving enthusiastically.

Isaac set his hand on Carson's knee and squeezed. "Looks like we're in this now."

Nodding, Carson waved back to her through the windshield. A pink hue flushed into his cheeks.

The older sister wrangled herself into a hammock hanging between two cedars. She held her drink out above her and managed to get in without spilling.

Isaac pulled in next to the grime-coated Ford Fusion. He figured they had to have a V-6 if they were pulling the pop-up with it. The younger of the two sisters was already at the truck's passenger side door before Isaac had even cut the engine.

She tried the handle and then pulled Carson's door open. "Thank God, you came! I was getting so bored. I didn't think you'd come." She wore a t-shirt and ripped-knee jeans. As Ashley always had at that age, she wore makeup as though ready for a day at the mall rather than one spent around a smoldering campfire.

Carson looked at her and then looked down into his hands in his lap. "Hey, Carly."

Isaac wasn't sure of his next move. Dropping his fifteen-year-old son off with two strangers didn't seem like the best idea. Then again, if he lingered too long, he could ruin the vibe and have Carson resenting him. He decided he'd stay long enough to get the lay of the land. He needed to get a bead on the older sister. The younger seemed harmless enough, if not a little overzealous. Isaac opened his door, stepped down, and stretched his back.

"Let me show you our camper," Carly said. She dragged a docile, though enchanted, Carson by the hand.

Isaac almost protested, but then, what was really going to happen? Were they somehow going to have sex in one of the wings of the pop-up without him noticing?

With the door still hanging open, they disappeared inside.

"Mosquitos!" the older sister called out from the hammock.

Carly's arm appeared, grabbed the handle to the pop-up door, and slammed it closed.

"Thank you!"

"You're welcome," Carly called back, her voice honeyed with sarcasm equal to her sister's.

Isaac started toward the hammock. Carly was doing most of the talking inside the pop-up with the occasional "That's cool" coming from Carson. Isaac cleared his throat when he was within five feet of the older sister.

She turned her head from whatever she'd been looking at across the lake. Her gaze traced up Isaac from his feet to his face. She offered a small smile. "Oh, the dad. I guess I thought he'd driven himself over."

He raised his hand. "Hi. I'm Isaac...like you say, the dad." He sniffed in a breath and rubbed a finger across the stubble of his upper lip. "He drives, but it's pretty easy to get turned around on these dirt roads and two-tracks."

She studied him a moment longer with her green eyes. "Morgan," she said.

Her name...she was introducing herself. Isaac nodded, feeling fuzzy again as he had in the morning when waking. It couldn't be called a hangover, but the edible had left him groggy. He was slow on the uptake. "Oh, good to meet you, Morgan. This is a great spot. I always wanted to camp here when I was younger, but for fishing it always seemed to make more sense to set up in one of the sites close to the Pigeon or the Black."

"The Pigeon River," she said, musingly. "It sounds better in Ojibwa. Meeme Sibi." She pursed her lips around the straw and sucked in a drink. She swallowed. "I guess back in the day, this area was quite the draw for wild pigeons." She sat up and swung her feet over the edge to the ground. Pulling the celery rib from her mug, she snapped off a bite and tossed the rest over her shoulder. "Can I make you a bloody mary?" she said while still chewing.

Isaac wondered if she was old enough. "I don't drink," he said.

"That must make it difficult to stay hydrated." She smiled. "And I'm 21."

"Hmm?"

"You just had a look on your face. No worries, it's legal for me to drink."

Isaac shook his head. "Not at all." From inside the pop-up came the sounds of dice on a laminate tabletop.

"Yahtzee." Carson didn't deliver the word gloatingly as he would have with his sisters. Instead, he sounded good sportsmanly, if not slightly apologetic.

"Sounds like they're hitting it off," Isaac said. "Playing games already."

Morgan glanced back at the camper and then to him. "He should come back tonight. Carly brought her telescope. We're hoping that the clouds clear off."

Isaac put his hands in his pockets. He rocked up on his toes and then back down to flat feet. "We're actually going to be packing up and heading back south."

She studied him for a moment. "That's too bad. I know she's enjoying the company. If it's just the two of us for too long, we drive each other crazy." She took another pull, and her straw rasped hollowly as she sucked the last of her drink up into it. She hopped out of the hammock and started for the camper. "I'm going to get a refill." Midstride, she stopped and turned to him. "Are you staying?" The question didn't have the sound of an invitation in it.

At least her second drink? Could even be a third or fourth. He decided to linger a little bit to see if he could really trust her being in charge. He looked at a stump where someone from the ranger's station had cut down what had probably been a dead or dying tree in the campsite. He made to sit down on it. "I'll stay for a bit."

"Yahtzee!" Carson said again with a little more enthusiasm in his voice.

"That's two times," Carly said. "You're cute *and* lucky."

Morgan looked toward the pop-up, shook her head, and then looked back to Isaac. "She speaks her mind...doesn't really play her cards close to her chest." Then she pointed at Isaac. "What about coffee?"

Isaac nodded. "Sure. Black is fine."

"That's good because that's all we have. I don't trust people who pollute good coffee with cream and sugar." She opened the door and stepped up into the camper. She closed the door behind her.

The dice continued their tumbling from inside. Isaac looked out over the lake reflecting the overcast sky. Slight breezes sent ripples across it. In the middle, a fish came up for an insect, and the ring it started expanded over the surface before disappearing.

"Yahtzee!" Carson said. "I can't believe that."

"You should go into town and get a lottery ticket," Morgan said flatly.

Isaac looked back at the pop-up and smiled.

Morgan said something else, but it was indiscernible.

"Okay," Carly said, as though she'd been scolded. "Want to call it a draw and go down by the lake?" she asked.

"A draw?" Carson said, exasperated but good naturedly. "In what world—"

"I'm kidding," she said, laughing. "You won. Let's go down and see if we can find some skipping stones."

Isaac smiled again. Playing Yahtzee and then skipping stones. It was exactly the kind of concrete experiences he'd hoped Carson would have while camping. Why hadn't he thought to bring any games for them to play?

Carly bounced out of the camper with Carson in tow. She had the fingers of her left hand laced into the fingers of his right. Smiling dumbly, he trailed along slightly behind her like a grateful stray she'd found and was bringing home.

Carson looked toward Isaac. It was a look that said, "What are you still doing here?"

"Just having some coffee," Isaac said, answering the look.

"We're going down to the lake," Carson said, coldly.

Isaac nodded. "Have fun." He watched them make their way down the gradual slope that would lead them to the water's edge. Carson looked back a couple times. Each look was an indictment.

Isaac swatted a dismissive hand in Carson's direction.

Morgan pushed the camper door open with her foot. She held identical metal coffee mugs in each hand, the only difference being the steam coming from one and then celery poking up from the other. She caught the door again with her foot and swung it closed.

"Not going to be super fresh, but it's kinda hot." She handed him the mug. "Sorry if there are any grounds. I tried to strain them."

"Long as it's caffeinated," he said, taking the mug from her. He blew across the surface and then took a cautious sip. Bitter, but still good. Down near the water, Carson and Carly were hunched over with scanning the shoreline for flat stones. Isaac took in a deep breath and exhaled. "Feels good to get out in the woods, doesn't it?"

Morgan sat in the zero-gravity chair, but didn't recline, keeping her feet planted on the ground. She pointed toward Carly. "I like to get her out camping for a week or so at least once a summer."

He nodded. "That's what I'm doing with him. I just think teenagers spend way too much time on their phones." He watched Carson wrist a stone at the surface that skipped three times before sinking. "They need a little time with Mother Nature," Isaac said.

Morgan laughed.

"What?"

She took a drink and then rested the mug on her knee. "I just always find it funny the impulse to anthropomorphize nature. It doesn't care about us, nor should it given the way people treat it."

Isaac took another sip of his coffee. "What's anthropo-whatever you said?"

"Anthropomorphize. It just means treating something that isn't human as though it's human. Like the idea that nature is a mother to people." She took another drink.

"If that's the case, then humanity is one abusive and neglectful child."

Isaac nodded. Listening to her reminded him of listening to his wife in the past. Gwen would get going on topics and hit him with vocabulary and metaphors that often left his head spinning.

"I won't argue with you that we don't treat nature all that good." He looked towards the kids. Carly sent a stone across the water. Isaac lost count after it had skipped over ten times. Surprising him, she jumped into Carson's arms in celebration. Carson held her awkwardly. Good God, Isaac thought, does she think he has a trust fund or something? Were teens simply that forward now? He turned back to Morgan. "What do your folks do?"

"My mother is deceased. My father is retired and living with his whore. Carly stays with me as often as she can. We are all in the Flint area." She took a longer drink. "I attend the University of Michigan. Of course, anyone in Ann Arbor would say, 'You attend the University of Michigan... *Flint*,' with an emphasis on the distinction."

"People can be snobs." Isaac cleared his throat. "Sounds like you don't really get along with your stepmother." He wondered how his kids would react to him bringing someone into his life. Whore seemed a little harsh.

"Please don't use any form of the word 'mother' when referring to that...woman. As far as I'm concerned, she's a gold digger and a walking depository of numerous venereal diseases."

Isaac sniffed out a laugh. "Okay, then. We can change the subject." He took another bitter sip. His mind drifted to

Emily. He tried to imagine her doing what Morgan had done. Packing for a trip? Hitching a camper up to a car? Towing a camper on the interstate? For that matter, driving a car at all. Emily was older than Morgan and, by comparison, seemed powerless. Thinking of her always left him feeling not that he had a daughter but instead was inextricably connected to someone he needed to save. He shook off his oppressive thoughts and focused on Morgan. "How often do you and your sister come here to camp?"

For the first time, Morgan glanced toward the teens. Then she looked back to Isaac. "We've never been here before. I wrote a paper about this area for my Michigan History course in the winter semester. Carly brought up our annual trip, so I thought, why not come here. I had to read about the place for 10 weeks, so I thought I might as well see it. I might do a little first-hand research."

Isaac looked around at the woods and water before looking back to her. "It's really something what they've done with this forest. I mean, like you say, people have been less than good to nature, but this..." He waved his hand around, gesturing to the trees, the lake, the sky. "...there's not a lot of stories like this in the history of conservation. A win for nature and for people."

She smiled sardonically over the rim of her drink. "For most people," she said. She sucked in another mouthful through the straw. "It's a checkered history. Like most history with this country, there's always a hint of displacement."

Isaac nibbled his lower lip. "Here? It was my understanding that the land was largely undesirable. Not much timber left to speak of, and the soil wasn't right for farming."

Morgan flicked the rim of her mug, which offered a dull chime. "Almost makes you wonder why they didn't relocate a Native American tribe here. I mean, that tended to be the way, didn't it? Give them the garbage." She took a drink and then sniffed in a breath. "It couldn't have been that undesirable. If you look at a map of the forest, you'll see more than a dozen areas that indicate private land."

Isaac thought of the handful of cabins along the Black River upstream from where he and Carson were camping. "I suppose a few properties were grandfathered in," he conceded. "Or whatever they did to keep their property."

She nodded, smirking. "Just need to have the right grandfather."

Isaac crossed his arms. "I'm not sure I follow."

"Not everybody who was on this land wanted to leave. Connection to a geography can be about more than how much money that land can generate, even if that is antithetical to capitalist thinking." She pushed her straw aside and took a long drink that had her tilting her neck so the dregs would slide down her throat. When she looked at him again, she wore a faint shadow of bloody mary mustache. She licked it away. "With enough harassment and a few intentional forest fires, almost anyone can be persuaded to give up their land."

Isaac leaned forward. "Are you saying that Native Americans were run off?"

She shook her head. "No, not Native Americans. From what I could find, it was religious persecution, but their faith lacked specifics. They'd come from the East Coast, blended and even co-mingled for a time with other obscure religious groups in northwestern Lower Michigan, and then one sect, I guess you would say, bought hundreds of acres in an area that now includes the ranger's station. They'd established a commune of sorts. From what I understand the locals didn't like them...you know, the whole 'they aren't like us' bullshit."

Isaac raised his eyebrows. "I hadn't heard anything about that."

"The winners write history," she said, shrugging one shoulder. "One incident was very likely murder, but the Gaylord Herald Times article reported it as an accidental death due to fire. It wasn't long after that death of one of their own, I guess a leader of sorts, that the people in question moved off the land. I guess they could see the writing on the wall."

"How would you figure it as a murder?"

She reached over the side of her chair and set her mug on the ground. "I don't think it was anyone of authority or connected with the efforts to establish the state land." She laced her fingers together and cracked her knuckles. "It was most likely some locals who used the forest rehabilitation as an excuse to drive off a group of people that they found undesirable." She shook her head. "That was no accidental death. The circumstances were just too suspicious."

Quite a few S sounds in that sentence. She'd slurred over a few of them.

"I think I've had enough." She must have heard the slurring too. "Those bloody marys go down a little too easy."

Given his history, he couldn't really say anything. At least she wasn't headed straight into the pop-up to fix another one.

He crossed his arms. "Almost any booze went down a little too easy for me."

"Oh," she started, looking at him inquisitively, "you're in recovery. I guess I thought you were just a teetotaler."

He hadn't heard that word in some time. He shook his head. "Nope. I had a problem, and I had to quit. Probably one of the best things I've ever done for myself." He looked around them again at the trees and then down to the teens who were wading in water up to their knees. Carson had his pant legs rolled and looked like he could be in some Norman Rockwell painting called *Looking for Crayfish* or something to that effect. Isaac looked back to Morgan. "Overall, though, you have to admit that they did a good job making this place as pure and public as possible."

"Ah, yes," Morgan said, "the 'Big Wild'... except, of course, for the oil derricks. But maybe they were grandfathered in?" She smiled callously.

He shrugged. "It's hard to get in the way of Shell Oil."

Morgan laughed disdainfully. "It's hard to get in the way of *money*. Period. Everything else, including people's lives, is negotiable. The morals of this country make me sick." She reached down for her mug but then seemed to remember that it was empty. She brought her hand back up into her lap. "They drive off people who were essentially living in harmony with nature, but they still allow oil drilling that puts that very nature at risk." She looked again toward Carly and Carson.

She wasn't wrong. He'd made an entire career of helping to abate an inadvertent accident of progress, though accident seemed too small a word. Tragedy was probably the better description. It started with man-made canals and locks in the 1800s. As a result, evidence of sea lamprey turned up in Lake Ontario as early as the 1830s. Then in the early 20th Century, shippers wanted a way around Niagara Falls for access to the upper Great Lakes. Enter the Welland Canal, which bypassed the falls for ships and, tragically, for lamprey.

Evidence of sea lamprey in the four other Great Lakes soon followed. Lake Erie, 1921. Lake Michigan, 1936. Lake Huron, 1937 and, finally, Lake Superior, 1938. In the name of shipping or, as Morgan noted, in the name of money, a 94,000 square-mile ecosystem was irrevocably changed, like accidentally giving a patient the wrong blood type. Even his division within the Fish & Wildlife Service used language like "abatement" because eradication of the invasive species was impossible. The vampires of the Great Lakes were there to stay, feeding off and endangering the native fish population for the rest of time.

Isacc took a drink of his coffee. It had started to go cold, and he could feel the grit of the grounds between his teeth. He examined the contents of the mug. Gray flecks floated on the surface. He poured it out next to the side of the stump. "I think that's about spent."

Morgan glanced at the spot where the coffee was soaking into the ground. "It was okay, though? You had some?"

Isaac nodded while yawning. "I did. Woke me up a little bit, but apparently not enough."

"Dad, can we stay?"

Isaac turned to see Carson and Carly, hand in hand, walking up the rise back into the campsite. "I guess I'm willing to stay a bit longer." He wasn't sure how much more of Morgan's self-righteousness he could take.

Carson shook his head. "No, I mean stay camping, like stay through to Friday morning like we planned or at least until tomorrow evening. Carly's setting up a telescope tonight, and tomorrow they are going to some different elk viewing areas."

Isaac smiled knowingly. "Thought you didn't want to go elk viewing."

"Dad."

Isaac stood up and yawned into his hand. What was the hurry to get home? Emily didn't want him there. Carson clearly liked the girl. He remembered his own first crushes. Those moments of liking someone and that someone liking you in return. At that age, it felt like everything that ever was important. He wasn't going to deprive his son of that, a few nights of terrible sleep be damned. Not to mention, he could get some more fishing in. Isaac nodded. "We can stay. I'll drive you back here later this evening for a few hours while I fish. But right now, we gotta scoot so I can try to get a nap in. I'm exhausted."

Carly let go of Carson's hand. Carson looked down at the absence of her fingers in his own. He looked back to Isaac. "Or I could just stay right now. You can go sleep and then fish and pick me up tonight."

Isaac shook his head. "No, we should head back for a bit. I'll make us some dinner after a nap." He looked at his son. "Let's get in the truck, bud. Chop-chop."

Carson crossed his arms. "I'm not really hungry."

Morgan spoke before Isaac could say anything. "He's welcome to eat with us later. Just going to make some hobo pies over the fire."

Carson looked at her and then snapped his hopeful expression back to Isaac.

Isaac shook his head again. "Thanks, but no. We'll go and regroup before I bring him back later."

Carson shrugged his hands into the air in front of him. "Regroup? Why are you being such a dick?"

Isaac took a step back. "What did you say?"

"Carly…" Morgan said, her tone scolding.

Carly looked at her sister and then back to the standoff between father and son. "Carson," she started. Her voice was calm and just above a whisper. "Go with your dad. Don't be disrespectful. I'll be here waiting for you."

Carson looked at her, nodded, and then went to the truck and opened the passenger door.

Isaac watched him before turning back to their hosts. He shook his head. "I guess he's not going to say goodbye."

"It's fine," Carly said. "He was telling me about how tense things can get back at home between you and Emily. He carries a lot of stress about it."

Isaac stared at her. He blinked. Carson was already talking with her that openly? The most Isaac could ever get out of him was, "I'm fine." What else was he not telling him? Isaac swallowed. "Yeah," he said, "I guess it has been a little tense." When he smiled, his upper lip buckled in against his teeth. "It was good to meet both of you." He looked at Morgan. "Thanks for the coffee and conversation." He looked at Carly. "I'll drive him back here around seven or so."

"Thank you, Mr. Fletcher. For what it's worth, he said he's having a good time camping with you."

"Thanks, Carly." He turned and started for the truck. Moments earlier, he'd been ready to climb into the driver's seat and express a few choice words to his son. After listening to Carly, he wasn't sure what he should say. He probably hadn't really thought enough about how the strained home environment might be affecting Carson.

He opened the door, climbed up into the truck, and closed the door again. He gripped both hands on the wheel but didn't turn the engine over. "We good?"

Carson pulled his gaze from looking out into the trees. "What?"

Isaac exhaled. "I know things aren't great with your sister and me, but I don't care for the name-calling."

"What are you talking about?"

Isaac nodded and waved his hand through the air in front of him. "You're right. Let's forget it." With a twist of his wrist, he started the truck. "But let's not let it happen again."

Seeming preoccupied, Carson turned back to the window. "Okay. Whatever."

Isaac sniffed in a sharp breath. Navigating the truck back out from the campground, he looked in his rearview mirror. Carly was climbing into the hammock. Morgan kneeled near the stump where Isaac had sat. She seemed to be examining something on the ground, sifting through the dirt with a stick. He watched her in the small reflection until he rounded a corner, and she disappeared from his sight.

CHAPTER 9

In the afternoon, after they came back from Town Corner Lake and had a snack of summer sausage with crackers and cheese, Isaac climbed into his cot and tried to sleep. It wasn't easy. He rolled from his back to his side to his other side and then on his back again. Even with the window flap open, the air in the tent seemed stale and somehow lacked enough oxygen. Despite no sunshine, the polyester gave the inside of the tent a stifling greenhouse effect. Outside, Carson was restless and, after a time, began thwacking his target with arrows. It was likely a passive-aggressive move that said, "I wanted to stay with Carly, and you wanted to sleep, so I guess we're both out of luck." If Isaac had dozed at all, it hadn't done much to make him feel rested. He finally abandoned the tent and proposed taking Carson back to Carly's campsite a little early.

Of course, Carson was more than receptive. It's what he'd wanted from the jump. Why didn't I just leave him there? Isaac wondered. He would have been fine. Was Isaac a little jealous of the teen's instant connection with Carly? Sure. Was it fair to pull a power move on the kid just to show him that his old man was still in control? Probably not.

It was just after six when they climbed into the truck. Carson's cheeks flushed red when Isaac asked him if he had a condom.

"What? Dad," he said, "we're not going to have sex. Jesus."

Isaac regripped the steering wheel. The truck's tires climbed over the root-woven two-track. "And I'm in no way saying that you should. You just need to be prepared." He stifled a yawn into the back of his hand. "It's easy for things to get carried away."

Carson turned to look out his window. "Man, that escalated quickly. You always do that...right to the drama. You might have started by asking if I've ever kissed anybody."

Isaac swallowed. "Well, have you?"

"No."

Isaac stared straight ahead through the windshield. "Is there anything you'd want to ask me about that?"

"Again, no. If it happens, I'm sure I'll figure it out. You're making it awkward."

Isaac drove for a moment in silence. Somehow, he felt he'd ruined a moment where they might have been able to bond. What useful he could have told him about kissing, he wasn't certain. Maybe he did escalate things too quickly. He thought he was doing the right thing by bringing up condoms. Was that why his kids could sometimes be reticent with him? Were they too concerned that he'd blow things out of proportion?

Looking ahead, Isaac slowed the truck to a stop in the middle of the road. He pointed through the windshield to the southern distance where overhead powerlines and a procession of utility poles cut a long clearing through the woods before turning out of sight to the east. "Look," he said.

A hundred yards down the powerline trail, a bull elk stood looking in their direction. The dark fur of its face, neck and legs contrasted against the lighter coat of its body. From the distance, it was hard to tell, but Isaac knew that it likely stood about five feet at the shoulders and weighed over 800 pounds. After a moment, it turned its profile toward them, showing a silhouetted rack of antlers that resembled a long crown of thorns resting on its head and supported on its back.

"Whoa," Carson said.

Isaac smiled at his son's one syllable exclamation. "I know, right? I probably sound like a broken record saying this, but they make a deer look like a dog."

The elk glanced their way one more time before walking casually west into the woods towards the river. In moments it was gone.

"Well, you got to see one."

Carson nodded. "I hope we do again. I want Carly to see one. She'll go crazy."

Isaac shook his head. Carson talked about her like he'd known her for years, not hours. He shifted the truck back into drive and started toward Town Corner Lake. They drove for a minute in silence.

Isaac scratched the back of his neck. He remembered his first girlfriend in high school when he was a sophomore and she a senior. They'd never gone all the way so to speak but had done their fair share of making out. She'd been open about what she liked and what she didn't. He glanced at Carson looking pensively out his window. Then he turned back to the road. He cleared his throat. "Look, if you end up kissing, just go slow. Take your cues from her. If your tongue does get involved, just remember that you're not trying to reach her tonsils."

"Dad."

Isaac shrugged. "I'm just saying." He turned toward his son. The teen stayed with his face turned toward his window. The tip of his left ear was flushed red. Isaac figured they'd talked enough about kissing.

When they arrived at the girls' campsite, Isaac noticed that Morgan had cleaned herself up. She wore jeans and a flannel shirt with the sleeves rolled. Her hair was tied back in a ponytail with a bandana. As far as he could tell, she wasn't drinking, at least not anything more than the Coke she was holding. They talked for a moment about the plans with the telescope and where they hoped to set it up.

"And it's okay if it's somewhere between 10:30 and 11 when I pick him up?" Isaac asked.

"That's not a problem at all. We stay up quite late," she said. "And, be assured, I will be keeping a close eye on them." Her tone suggested that she had her own concerns about the two of them possibly getting a little too frisky.

"I appreciate that," Isaac said.

After saying his goodbyes, he drove back to the dispersed campsite and took another shot at lying in the cot. A mourning dove cooed softly at the periphery of the site. A half hour later, on the verge of falling asleep, he instead sat up at the sound of a vehicle's tires crunching down the two-track towards him. He looked out through the screen. One of the ranger's trucks was slowing to park in the long grass. Isaac swung his legs to the ground and pulled his shoes on. The ranger was out of the truck and walking towards him just as Isaac climbed out of the tent.

"Hey," Isaac said. "Everything good?"

The man introduced himself as Branson Strang, the head ranger. His salt and pepper mustache was matched by salt and pepper hair parted down the middle and feathered back on the sides. His eyes were icy blue. Broad-shouldered and barrel-chested, he looked like he'd been ordered out of a ranger catalog.

"I'd heard someone was in this site," Strang said. "Off the road and out of sight down here, I like to check in sometimes... you know, make sure everything is a-okay."

"Everything is fine here." Isaac smiled and nodded. "If anything, just tired. Getting a little old for this sleeping on a cot in a tent business, but the site and the fishing have been pretty good."

"Good to hear. I like to be safe. Couple summers ago, a guy had a stroke, and it was a few days before we found him." Strang put his hands in his pockets.

Isaac scratched above his eyebrow. "Somebody died here?"

Strang shook his head. "No, he still had a pulse when we found him. He died at the hospital in Gaylord. Sad stuff." He glanced around at the site. "You're here by yourself?"

Isaac shook his head. "No, I'm with my son. He's over visiting a friend's campsite at Town Corner Lake."

"Gotcha." Strang looked around the site. "You got other kids?"

"Not here with me, but my youngest daughter is back at home, and my oldest is in Muskegon with her husband. They are expecting their first." He nodded. "Soon, actually."

"Pregnant?" Strang's thoughtful look turned into a smile. "So, a first-time grandpa then?"

"Yup. Looking forward to it. What about you? Do you have kids?"

"Daughters. But no babies on the way yet, knock on wood. They'd be a little young for that." He smiled.

"I hear ya."

Strang nodded toward Isaac's truck. "That the only vehicle you have here?"

"Yup."

Strang nodded again absently. "And you're staying through until Friday?"

Isaac smacked the flat of his hand into a mosquito on his cheek. "Probably leaving Thursday before dark." He lifted it from his face and looked at his palm. Empty. He'd missed.

"Leaving tomorrow? Your tag says Friday."

Isaac shrugged. "We may stay until Friday. Is that going to be a problem if we do end up leaving early?"

Strang shook his head no. "It's not like people are lined up to get into this site, anyway. No vault toilet and no water, it's just a little too rustic for most people."

They talked for a few minutes about the challenges and joys of rustic camping. Then, Strang said he needed to get back to the headquarters.

Isaac watched the ranger's taillights leaving through the grove of trees until he couldn't see them anymore. He went back into the tent. He closed his eyes just to rest them and, when he opened them again, it was dusk. Yes, he thought. I got some sleep. He rose quickly and loaded his fly-fishing gear into the back of the truck.

Five minutes later, Isaac parked in a sugar sand turnout where southbound Chandler Dam Road turned sharply eastbound. Just across the road and down a slope, the Black flowed southerly and, as he remembered, it widened out of a football field's worth of riffles into a broad, slow stretch that he'd referred to as The Flats in his youth. During the day, The Flats would be the kind of water that he would wade right through without even flicking a fly towards the shadowed edges. The water was too shallow and bright, and whatever fish were holed up under the banks stayed there out of cautious instinct. Under cover of darkness, however, they came out to feed in that oxygenated, slow current that made taking insects from the surface that much easier.

He recalled the night in his late twenties when he had discovered The Flats. On his first cast, he'd hooked an 11-inch brookie. Reeling it in and netting it, he slipped it into his wader pocket. He could feel it flopping against his stomach when he cast and immediately had another good-sized fish on. When their feeding frenzy had died off a half hour later, Isaac kneeled at the shore and slowly gutted the three keepers he'd taken from The Flats, smiling broadly in the moonlit night.

Leaving his memories in the cab, Isaac opened his door and stepped down from the truck. He closed the door and then, fists pressed into his lumbar, he stretched his back. He turned and looked to the south to the powerline trail where he and Carson had spotted the elk earlier. Of course it wasn't there, but some part of him had looked with anticipation. Nature's gifted moments were fleeting and almost never repeated.

Somewhere in the wilderness to the west, a family of coyotes yipped and howled. They were either calling the family together or giving a warning to another pack that might be getting too close. As a coda to their high-pitched ruckus, a final deeper howl filled the evening. Isaac guessed it was the alpha having the last word.

Isaac locked the truck and tucked his keys up into the hollow space behind his rear bumper. Taking his fly rod, he crossed the road and then eased down the bank and into the water. Looking downstream through a web of overhanging branches, he could see the head of The Flats where the rippling water turned to glass. He worked his way downstream toward it.

Wanting to take a moment to check for signs of feeding, he waded toward the left bank where logs lay pale in the light of the gibbous moon. Something small behind him scurried off through the rushes and deeper into the woods. Isaac pushed his palm down on a bigger log to test its stability before turning and sitting on it. His feet stirred up the thick muck near the shoreline. A pungent odor rose up from the surface. Even in the half-dark he could see the plumes of black silt rising around his calves, darkening the water. He turned his head and scanned The Flats for any signs of feeding fish.

Nothing.

Deciding that he would wait until he saw at least one rise, he reached into the front pocket of his waders and pulled out his phone. When he checked the time—9:27—he also noticed that he had a text. Strange that it hadn't made any noise. Hadn't he switched his phone to airplane mode? Maybe he hadn't and instead had just silenced it. He shook his head, ever more aware that his memory was starting to glitch as he aged. His battery was down to 13 percent.

The text was from Emily: *What's my blood type?*

A vexing sensation like a low-grade fever rose up Isaac's spine and spread over the surface of his skin. His gums itched, and his world shrank down to the words on his screen glowing like a mysterious prophecy in the darkness around him. Blood type? What did it mean? Of course, she couldn't do anything selfless like provide a context. His mind went immediately to an image of her in an emergency room on a red-stained gurney experiencing heavy blood loss from some household accident. Would they even do a blood transfusion without knowing her blood type? Was it a life-or-death question? Was she just being curious like she could sometimes get? How bad could it be if she was able to text? Suddenly needing to know her blood type had somehow become more important than anything, including her father's peace of mind.

His course of action simmered in him, leaving an emptiness in his stomach. Looking downstream absently, he nibbled his lower lip. He'd have to bag the fly fishing for the night and drive into Vanderbilt. First, he'd have to stop by Town Corner Lake and pick up Carson. The kid wouldn't be happy. It was very possible that they'd be making an emergency drive down to some hospital in Bay City or Saginaw. He sat for a moment in a fugue while his mind processed and then reprocessed the logistics of the next 24 hours. Was he really going to drive all the way into town because of a benign text?

Something flew into the branches some twenty feet above him. Staring at the message on his screen, he spotted it. He couldn't believe it. He adjusted his glasses and looked again. Somehow, he had two bars of connection. Had they put up more cell towers closer to the state forest in the years since he'd been there? He'd never in all his past trips had more than a single rogue bar of reception. Normally the thought of more cellular service while in the outdoors would have left him disappointed, but the sudden reception came as something like divine intervention.

He stood, hoping that standing would better help him keep the connection. How many times had he seen his girls holding their phones above their heads to get a signal? Getting one call through could change the trajectory of the entire night. His feet settled slowly into the thick mud. He waited to touch down against some long-submerged branches, but instead his feet kept slowly sinking. In the western horizon, the silhouette of some night bird flew across the blue-black sky. Isaac pressed the thumbnail of Emily's picture and then the call icon.

She picked up after two rings. "Dad? Why are you calling?"

He could hear Harper in the background, laughing and then shouting something from another room. The Smiths were playing through the Bose speakers. The girls must have gotten into Gwen's old box of CDs. He couldn't name the song, they'd never really been his kind of band, but the moaning melancholy of that lead singer was hard to mistake. He remembered a lyric about the stolid stench of death on the moors...something about child murders. Their songs had always struck him as unnecessarily morose, but they were among Gwen's favorites and so he'd tolerated them in the same way she had tolerated his obsession with Zeppelin.

He was washed with relief just from hearing Emily's untroubled voice. "Why am I calling? Jesus Christ, I thought they were wheeling you into surgery."

She didn't speak right away. The music on her end of the call dropped dramatically in volume. Harper went silent. "What?" Emily asked, coming back on the line, "Why would you think that?"

Was she starting to have problems with *her* memory? He looked toward the moon and then back across the water into the darkness of the opposite shore. "Because of your text. You can't send shit like that without any context."

She was quiet again. Then: "Because I told you I was asking for more hours at work? I thought you'd be thrilled."

He shook his head. "No, that last one you sent."

"I'm looking right at it. That is the last one I sent."

He took in an exasperated breath and then exhaled. He looked at his phone screen and then brought it back to his ear.

"I'm looking at it, too. 'What's my blood type?' That's what you asked. It's right there, plain as day."

"What are y— Oh my god..." She laughed. "That's from like a month ago. Harper's cohort was helping with a blood drive, and I was thinking about giving blood. It must have just come through. Texts do that sometimes."

"Jesus Christ, I thought you needed a blood transfusion or something."

"I'm fine. Harper and I are making popcorn and getting ready to watch *Plan 9 from Outer Space*. She's never seen it." She sniffed in a short breath. "She really likes it here."

He nodded, washed in relief. "Okay." He looked downstream to The Flats and smiled at a fingerling brook trout jumping above the surface.

"Are you in Vanderbilt right now?" Emily asked. "I hope you didn't drive all the way into town."

He shook his head. "No, somehow I got a signal out on the river." He shifted his sinking feet. The mud pulled like suction cups at his wading boots.

"Do you need to get back to fishing?"

He sucked his lower lip in between his teeth and watched for more rises. "Not immediately, but soon."

She cleared her throat. "Okay. Do you remember what we talked about? About Harper?"

"What?" he asked absently. "Not really, I guess. Should I?" His attention had turned downstream toward the shadowy movements in his peripheral vision. He blinked a few times to assure that it was happening. Four-legged shapes slinked out of the blackness of the shoreline and waded into the shallow water of The Flats. One. Two. Five. Seven. For a moment, he wasn't sure what he was witnessing. He'd never seen anything like it in all his nights spent on Michigan's rivers. His mind finally put the details together. It was a pack of coyotes crossing the stream. A mist he hadn't noticed earlier smoked off the surface and drifted around the shadows of the scavenger canines. There certainly wouldn't be any fishing The Flats until they decided to wander off and the sediment resettled. His heart raced at the sight of them.

"We were talking about me and Harper and where we might live," Emily said from her end of the call.

"What about it?" he half-whispered, still watching the skittish animals in the river. He shivered in the night's falling temperatures. Farther downstream, on the far side of The Flats where the river narrowed again into a faster run, a larger shadow paced in the current. The water broke in white flashes against its legs. Isaac had read that alpha coyotes could be better-sized, but this silhouette seemed at least twice as big as the others. Maybe this oversized coyote was the "wolf" everybody had been seeing. Instead of finishing crossing, the others in the pack walked slow circles in the shallows, sometimes stopping to lap up a drink. If he weren't talking to Emily, he'd have tried to get video of the moonlit scene.

"Why are you whispering, Dad?"

He cupped his hand close to the mouthpiece of his phone. "There's coyotes in the river about 50 yards from me. They're getting a drink."

"Oh," Emily said. "Be careful."

He smiled. "They scare pretty easy. I'm not too worried."

"Okay." Emily cleared her throat again. "So, Harper talked to her parents, and they are okay with it...I mean, as okay as they get."

"They're probably relieved," Harper stated flatly in the background of the call.

The alpha coyote stopped pacing and turned its gaze upstream, reflecting an amber eyeshine. Isaac went still except for his heart. He'd clearly been spotted. The distant, glowing eyes stayed fixed on him. A phrase came into his head from one of the zoology courses he'd taken. Tapetum lucidum. It was a reflective layer behind an animal's retina that made it easier for them to see at night. Isaac imagined what he looked like in the alpha's vision. He wondered if it was something like the green apparition world of his night vision goggles. He used to use them in his youth to get out to his deer blind in the darkest morning hours.

"Dad?"

What had she said? Something about parents and being okay. "Okay with what, Em? What are you getting at?" He wondered if maybe they'd scoped out an apartment. It made sense with all her talk about asking for more hours at work. Maybe they needed somebody to co-sign the lease. If that's where she was angling, it sounded like the beginning of a disaster. He'd lay out all this money, and in two months, she'd come back home with her tail between her legs. Somehow, he couldn't imagine a scenario in which he didn't end up getting stuck paying the remaining months of their rent. "Are you trying to ask me for something?"

Downstream, a few of the coyotes turned their head in his direction. Their yellow-green eyeshine reflected the moonlight. Hair bristled between their shoulders and along their back closer to the tail.

Shit, he thought. They were seeing him as a threat. He tried to take a step back and almost fell over with the way the muck held his feet. The rest of the pack trained their eyes on him after his jerky movements of catching himself from falling. Twenty-two orbs glowed in his direction.

"You said Harper could move in with us."

Like hackles on the spine of the river, the shadow of the alpha coyote rose up until it stood hunched on its hindlegs. Isaac shook his head. That couldn't be what he was seeing. The mist weaved around the other coyotes' tensed bodies. Isaac tried to step backwards again, but his feet held fast. His heart jumped like a fresh-caught trout dropped into his ribcage.

"Dad?"

Isaac's hand fell to his side, bringing the phone away from his ear with it. Panicked, he yanked his right boot free of the mud. He just barely kept himself from falling in. A coyote charged toward him out of the shallow water into the upstream riffles and then circled back to join the pack. Isaac's chest felt like someone was tightening a belt around his ribs. His lips went numb.

The alpha threw its head back in a deep howl that the others joined with a high-pitched, piercing cacophony of yowls. Isaac yanked at his leg. The mud gave nothing back and sucked on his calf like a mouth. Downstream, the alpha dropped down to all fours. As it stalked upstream, the others fell in, flanking him on either side.

"What is this?" Isaac muttered. He shot his hands up above his head and waved them back and forth. Make yourself big. Make noise. It was the advice he remembered being told should he encounter a bear while fishing. It was all he had. "Hey!" he shouted, his voice cracking. "Get out of here!"

The pack continued their deliberate advance.

Isaac pulled again, yanking his leg free. The force of his effort and the release sent him toppling down into the current. His right sleeve soaked instantly from wrist to shoulder. Ice-cold water rushed into his waders, down his back, and over his legs. "Goddamn it!" He managed to hold his phone up above the surface.

"Dad? Are you okay?" Emily's tinny voice tinkled above him.

Isaac looked at the predatory shadows advancing upon him. "Help!" he shouted. "Someone help! Help me!"

The coyotes kept their steady pace, soundtracked by a low series of growls, hisses, and barks.

Isaac crashed his arm down sending an arc of water toward the pack. "Jesus Christ, just get away! Go!"

The alpha howled again.

"Daddy!"

Tinny and disembodied, Emily's scream was primordial coming from the phone above him. A chill shot up his spine and settled between his shoulder blades. Night birds that had been singing in the distance went instantly quiet.

Something suddenly burst out of the trees on the left bank and crashed into the water, scattering the smaller, yelping coyotes in splashy pounces toward the opposite shoreline. The dark, massive form moved into the heart of the pack like something possessed. The violent thrashing and plunging were accompanied by the bugling of the cow elk careening into the alpha coyote. She reared back on her hind legs and rained down several cracking blows with her front hooves. Yelping, the alpha fled across the river into the tag alders of the western shore. The cow elk pursued him.

"Holy shit," Isaac whispered. He watched only for a moment before turning over to his knees and rising into an awkward run upstream. Water rushed down and settled around his feet. His quick, cold breaths felt like something he would have breathed in during the dead of winter. He didn't look back until he was all the way up to the get-out spot. Catching his wind, he looked downstream at the moonlit water flowing undisturbed again. The elk and coyotes were long-since gone, and nothing remained of the terrifying moment save for Isaac's memory of it. As his adrenaline receded, he retched but kept himself from throwing up. After a moment, he reached up and turned on his headlamp.

Climbing the bank, he stood in the middle of the dirt road under the haunting blue light of the moon. In time, he heard a small voice imploring him from his palm. He brought the phone up to his ear.

"Dad? Dad?"

"I'm here," he said. He took a breath. "I'm okay." He was wet and exhausted and not quite sure what had happened, but he wasn't hurt. He coughed up phlegm and spit it onto the dirt road.

"What happen...?" Emily's end went quiet. Then: "I'm sorry, Daddy. I just feel like I'm going to—"

"Emily?" He took the phone from his ear and looked at the black screen.

It was dead.

CHAPTER 10

The next morning, Isaac stood outside the gas station-market in Vanderbilt with his phone to his ear. He turned his attention to the adjacent street. A handful of cars drove by. He took a sip from his coffee. Fresh and just the right temperature, it was the only bonus of coming all the way into town just to make a phone call. Forty-five minutes earlier, Morgan and Carly had stopped by the campsite to pick up an eager Carson for elk viewing. Isaac probably could have skipped the phone call and the drive into town, Emily wouldn't have cared, but after the way the phone had died before they'd finished speaking the night before, he felt he needed to talk to her.

On the drive in, he'd plugged his cell into the charging cord coming from his cigarette lighter port. It was at nine percent when he climbed out of the truck, topped off his gas, and went into the market for coffee.

He took another sip. The gray overcast stretched across the sky looked as though it had been smeared there with a butter knife. To his left, in the near distance, two men on mountain bikes pedaled north on the rail trail. His call to Emily rang a fourth time.

Somebody picked up after the fifth ring. "Hello?"

"Emily?"

"Hello, Mr. Fletcher. It's Harper. Emily is still sleeping." She said it as though she were going to hang up right after saying it. Not rude, just matter of fact.

Isaac remembered that it was close to ten o'clock. "You could probably wake her up," he said. "She's expecting a call from me."

Harper was quiet for a moment. She took a breath through her nose and then exhaled slowly. "I don't want to do that," she said. "I think she needs the rest. She was really tired after getting off the phone with you last night."

Isaac squeezed his hand into a fist and then released it. "I appreciate that, but I'd like to talk to her."

"Is it urgent? If not, I can take a message."

What the hell? He shook his head. "I wouldn't say it's urgent, but I was supposed to check in this morning. I wanted to let her know that I'm okay and to see if everything there was okay."

"Everything here is good. I can tell her that you're fine." She sniffed a breath. "I'm not trying to be disrespectful, but I really believe that her body is telling her that she needs to sleep."

He tried not to be irritated. At least Emily had somebody in her life looking out for her well-being. "I just wanted to make sure that she wasn't worried about me," he said. He wondered if Harper knew the whole story or at least some of the story. If not, it would have sounded like they had been fighting over the phone, especially with the way Emily had screamed. "I got into a bit of a pickle on the river while she and I were talking. I might have scared her."

Harper cleared her throat. "She didn't seem scared, just very tired. She felt like you were safe."

"Look, would you just tell her—"

"Oh, there's the doorbell." She hung up.

He stood staring at the phone in his palm. With his battery already down to seven percent, there was no sense in calling back. It was hard to get anywhere with Harper, anyway. He hadn't told Carson specifics, but his plan was to pack up and get on the road by dinnertime. He could clear everything up with Emily when he arrived home. He wasn't sure of a diplomatic way to deliver the news, but his plan was to say no to the idea of Harper moving in with them. He had enough challenging people under his roof. Hanging up midconversation because someone was at the door? He shook his head. Knowing those girls, it was probably DoorDash. With both being skinny as sticks, he wasn't sure where they put it, but it seemed like they were constantly ordering fast food.

He glanced again toward the rail trail. An old woman stood in the middle of the asphalt that cut a black line through the center of the village. She wore an open housecoat over a long, stained t-shirt that displayed a yellow Looney Tunes character. Her thin, white legs disappeared into a pair of mud boots. Staring in his direction, she held what looked like some kind of energy drink. Isaac's skin tingled behind his ears.

She made no effort to hide her gawking. After a moment, he cupped his hand to his mouth. "Morning!" he shouted, smiling. He waved.

In reply, she turned around without acknowledging his gesture. With her back to him, she shuffled across a field of yellowed grass toward a neighborhood of overgrown lawns and asbestos-sided houses. One home had a rusted car with no tires sitting in a pyre of long grass.

Well, she's a charmer, Isaac thought. He stood for a moment with the phone in his hand. He wondered how long he'd get before his battery died if he were to give Ashley a call. After a time, he slid the phone back into his pocket. Even if he had a full battery, he knew he'd talk himself out of calling his eldest. He already leaned on her too much emotionally. With a baby due to arrive any time, she didn't need to play counselor to her father. She certainly didn't need to hear about his bizarre encounter with the coyotes. She needed peace and rest before her delivery day. I could use some peace and rest myself, he thought.

Isaac opened the door to his truck, climbed in, and started the engine. He plugged his phone into the cigarette lighter. Before pulling away from the pumps, he took a moment to consider the day ahead. Given his sudden connection with Carly, Carson wasn't going to be happy about the plans to leave early, but Isaac couldn't bring himself to care. Between the long, dark night of the edible and then those crazy coyotes, he'd had enough of the trip. Closing his eyes, he could still picture the cow elk charging to his rescue.

What a strange, strange night.

Not long after leaving Vanderbilt, he guided the truck effortlessly along the curves of Sturgeon Valley Road. Short of one logging truck that barreled past him, and a handful of oncoming cars, the roadway asked little of his attention, allowing his mind to wander. His hallucination of his brother he could chalk up to the edible, no matter how real it had felt. Consuming that damn thing was a mistake that wouldn't be repeated. The coyotes and the elk, though, still had him shaken. He couldn't help but somehow think their behavior might be connected to the strange man in the river, the dead raven, and then hearing his brother's voice while out on the stream. Something beyond the natural seemed at play. Something seemed to be telling him that they should leave... and soon.

But then was the behavior really that bizarre? He'd probably startled the coyotes at their normal watering spot. They were just being territorial. And, if he thought about it rationally, the elk didn't truly come to his rescue. More likely, it had come to cross the river at the shallow spot, saw the coyote pack acting threateningly, and then defended itself out of instinct. Or, even more likely, it had a calf on the other side of the river. Isaac had been a fortunate, though unintended, benefactor of a mother protecting her own.

Isaac knew that time spent in the woods meant experiencing nature on its terms. His sleeping in the past had been interrupted by families of raccoons rummaging through the contents left atop a picnic table. Another time, he'd woken in the morning to a funnel weaver spider's web woven in a corner of his tent just above his head. The little, stubbled legs of the arachnid stuck out at the edges of its diminutive abyss. The strangest time perhaps, he and his fishing partner had even had an emaciated cow elk wandering circles through the campground they were in. It carried its head tilted to the side and seemed unaware of their presence. As it turned out, a ranger had explained, the animal likely had a brain worm that blinded it in addition to other neurological effects. Wandering sightless in a nearby meadow, abandoned by the rest of the herd, it had likely followed the sound of their neighbor's generator up into the campground.

Even so, his unusual memories seemed eclipsed by the behavior of those coyotes the night before. When he had picked Carson up from Town Corner Lake later that night, Isaac hadn't mentioned anything about his terrifying evening. Instead, he had let Carson go on about Carly and their night together. They'd spent a great deal of time with her telescope trained on the moon.

"Wasn't it too bright to see much detail?" he had asked.

"She had a moon filter, so we could see the craters and mountains. She said those dark spots that people used to think were oceans are actually fields of lava."

"I told you that a long time ago."

"Yeah, but I actually *listen* to her," Carson had said, smiling.

He hadn't revealed whether they'd kissed or done anything else, but his son was clearly smitten. When they had returned to their campsite, Carson couldn't help but notice Isaac's wet pants and upside-down waders hanging on the clothesline. He had a good laugh when Isaac explained, without explaining why, that he had fallen in. He wasn't certain if he'd ever tell

Carson the full details. Hearing about some freak incident like that would probably make the kid swear off the outdoors altogether.

Isaac put both hands on the steering wheel as the truck rolled across the Pigeon River Bridge. Slowing, he looked upstream but saw only stream, no trace of the strange man standing in the current. His mind drifted back to the night before.

He and Carson had both been tired and turned in without making a fire. While getting ready for bed, Carson had chattered on about his excitement to go elk viewing the next day. Isaac wasn't sure what to attribute it to—maybe coming down from all the adrenaline—but he had fallen asleep soon after climbing into his own cot. His being able to sleep had been one of the evening's few kindnesses.

When the cracked blacktop of Sturgeon Valley Road became dirt, he slowed down. He regripped his hands on the steering wheel and ground some residual bit of breakfast between his teeth. Driving past it, he glanced down the two-track to the Witness Tree parking area. No sign of Morgan's car. A mile later, he investigated the parking lot of one of the smaller elk viewing turnouts. No cars there either. He remembered that some of the better elk viewing was farther north near Cornwall Lake. Made sense. That spot was the farthest from most of the campgrounds and human activity. Maybe that's where Carson and the girls had gone. He briefly considered trying to find them but then imagined how put out Carson would be with that kind of interloping.

Isaac soon turned down the two-track into their campsite. They were going to do what Carson had asked, which was to at least stay until the evening. Isaac imagined them coming back from elk viewing with big plans to catch fireflies or do some other nighttime activity. To be prepared for that contingency, his plan was to have most of the campsite broken down before the kids even returned. If the cots and tent were put away, it would be clear to Carson that they were leaving. "What?" Isaac imagined himself saying, "You said that you wanted to stay until at least Thursday evening. Well, it's Thursday evening."

If Carson wanted to see more of Carly, he'd have to get her contact information. Hell, she was only down in Flint, about 45 minutes from their place. They'd be going down that way for Carson's archery competition in October. Isaac suspected, though, that Carson would want to see her much sooner than that. Or, as these things often did, it would fizzle on its own. In any case, that was Carson's to figure out. Hunched over, Isaac began circling the tent and popping the plastic hooks that held the rain fly in place.

Within forty-five minutes, he had nearly everything packed into the truck. Seeing it as a chance to instill responsibility, he left the archery equipment for Carson to handle. Isaac had left one of the bag chairs out sitting by the cooler. On top of the cooler, a paper plate with cheese and crackers sat next to a can of diet pop. Isaac dropped himself down into the chair. With his right hand he stacked a square of cheese onto one of the wheat crackers from his little pile. In his left hand, he held a copy of *Walden*, one of Gwen's favorite books. He was going to try to do what he'd always imagined would be a good afternoon activity while camping.

He was going to try to read.

While chewing, he opened to the first page and leaned back into the chair. He propped his feet up on a stump. Before starting, he turned the book over and looked at the back cover. No pictures...just more words. He reached over absently and dropped another piece of cheese onto a cracker.

Before reading it, he took in the length of the first sentence again. Jesus Christ, eight commas? Where the hell was the period? It wasn't the first time he'd tried to read the book. Isaac had much preferred the Hemingway stuff Gwen had suggested for him, especially the fly-fishing stories. A favorite of his was "Big, Two-Hearted River." Nick Adams, heart sick from what he's seen during World War I, goes to Michigan's Upper Peninsula for a restorative fly-fishing trip. He carries a darkness in his soul that his realignment through nature helps him start to release. Isaac had read the novella several times.

Nevertheless, Gwen had always wanted him to read *Walden*. "Thoreau says a lot of the same stuff you say, just differently," she'd said. As many times as he'd taken it with him while out in the field for lamprey abatement work, he'd never gotten past the first few pages.

He held the book up toward the sky. "I'm giving it another shot, honey," he said softly.

Fifteen minutes later, he closed the book. He looked at his plate of crumbs. He'd absently eaten all of his snack. "I'm sorry, honey," he said, looking up to the sky again. He had read the first five pages of tiny print. The sentences were thick and the vocabulary often over his head. Not knowing the meaning of a word or two often kept him from the meaning of entire sentences. There was talk of Sandwich Islanders and Brahmin and being suckled by wolves. The way people are living is a self-imposed misery, Thoreau seemed to be saying, but Isaac couldn't imagine a more difficult way to say it.

Making room in the bed of the truck, he packed in the cooler and the bag chair. Then, he walked over to the clothesline. Pulling them down, he reached deep into one of his wader legs until his fingers were probing the insides of the stocking booty. It had largely dried out. The idea came to him that he could get out for one more afternoon fish. The attempt the night before had been a wash. He hadn't even tried one real cast. That morning, he had skipped fishing altogether to drive into town, only to be rebuffed by Harper. On a brighter day, fishing a dry fly in the early afternoon would have been just about pointless. Looking up, he examined the sky. The cloud cover was in his favor. Middle of the day, too, he was certain that he wouldn't be running into any coyotes.

Even as he weighed the variables, he was already pulling his waders up over his legs. Next, his wader boots. Taking another good-sized fish from the river might be a salve for what otherwise had been a distressing trip...at least for him, not so much for lover boy.

When he'd finished getting ready to fish, he opened the passenger side door and took a pen from the glove box. He rummaged around the rest of the contents until he found a yellow piece of paper that some tree trimming company had left on his windshield to advertise their services. Checking the time, he noticed that he had one percent left on his phone's battery. It didn't matter. He could charge it on the drive home. On the back side of the advertisement, he wrote a note for Carson, explaining that he'd gone fishing and would be back by three o'clock. That would give him around two hours to fish. Satisfied with the note, he pinned it under the driver's side windshield wiper. Carson could be inattentive at times, but even he couldn't miss the bright yellow paper in an otherwise almost empty campsite.

Isaac followed the trail through the swampy tag alder and down into the river. For a time, he lost himself in the fishing. As he had hoped, the overcast sky had the brookies willing to feed off the surface despite the time of day. Nothing he hooked up with could go in the creel, but having consistent fish coming up after his fly proved to be its own distraction. A few of the seven and eight-inch fish gave him good fights, and he even smiled a little at their antics as they sprang thrashing from the surface or tried to break themselves off in the roots near the bank.

When he'd fished to the spot where he'd caught the keeper on their first evening, he took his phone out of his wader pouch. It was dead again. He guessed that he'd been fishing for a little over an hour. He could fish a few more bends and then get out on the east side of the river and trudge the road back to their site. He remembered a few spots downstream where past fishermen had already blazed makeshift paths through the trees out to Chandler Dam Road. He'd probably take some branches to the face or get turned around a time or two but choosing one of the lesser-used paths would keep him from getting too close to The Flats. Even in the middle of the day, he didn't want to see that stretch of water again any time soon. The thought of it gave him a chill. He suspected he'd eventually get over it.

He worked a corridor of tag alder, casting his fly under the reach of their lowest offshoots as best he could. A red-winged blackbird kept pace with him, flitting through the upper branches of the westside bank. Its swatches of blood-hued and yellow feathers flashed in his peripheral vision. In the near eastern distance, a vehicle going at a pretty good clip raced down Chandler Dam Road.

Around the next bend, the tag alder would thin, and the river would widen to 30 feet or so in width. He could picture the boulder in the middle of the stream that he remembered from fishing this stretch years before. He reeled in his line, blew drying breaths into the hackle of his fly, and then doused it again with floatant. With the shadowed cover it provided for fish, the boulder would likely be his last best chance to pick up a keeper before he'd have to get out.

As he rounded the bend, the red-winged blackbird flew across the river in front of him and then up and out of his sight to the east. Isaac looked downstream. For a moment, it was just that something was off. He was seeing something that shouldn't have been there. It wasn't a color he expected. Something large and black lay lodged against the boulder with the water breaking white against it. A plastic wheel spun, suspended in the air. He blinked. His brain fit together the discordant details like puzzle pieces.

The baby stroller. How did it end up—?

His head suddenly felt as though it were in a closing vice. The hip joint of his bad leg ached, and the hair on his arms rose to standing in response to the faint electricity charging the air. The barometric pressure was falling rapidly. A peal of thunder began in the southern distance but ended directly above him. Instantaneously, the wind raged through the branches of the tag alder and evergreens around him. A large tree fell somewhere behind him in the woods. It sounded like a thousand femurs breaking before the final whoosh of it coming to rest on the forest floor. Storm clouds poured across the sky from the south to the north, darkening the day to twilight. Then the rain came fast and hard. Isaac rushed to the shore and pressed himself into the protection of the mesh of branches, feeling the cold rain soaking through his clothes and over his skin. He looked out into what may as well have been television static above the surface of the river. His thoughts went to Carson and the girls. He'd taught his son how to take the right kind of cover in a storm.

Had he truly listened?

This is bad, Isaac thought, blinking at the rain gathering in his lashes. The crash of falling trees boomed around him from all directions. The wind sounded like jet engines.

This is really bad.

CHAPTER 11

After thirty minutes of climbing over and under fallen timber, Isaac stumbled out of the wet woods onto Chandler Dam Road. He was soaked through with rain and sweat. The sun had come out while he was still toiling through the trees and underbrush. It had been a brief respite before the cloud cover had flooded in again. The birds called excitedly to each other, reestablishing contact after the chaos of the storm. Touching his fingertips along the scratches on his face, Isaac realized that somewhere in his struggle a branch had ripped the fishing net from the back of his vest. He looked behind him at the wreckage of dripping woods. He shook his head. The net could be replaced.

Palms on his knees, he stood bent for a moment, catching his breath. Then, he lifted his head from its downward gaze and studied the road north back to the campsite. Washed out with puddles and crisscrossed with fallen branches and splintered limbs, what lay in front of him could hardly be called a road. He started trudging forward, threading himself through spaces he could find in the maze of deadfall. With many trees, entire root systems were jutting toward the sky in a spectacle of windthrow. It was rare for Michigan, but he figured it had to have been a twister that touched down. He recalled that in 2022, a tornado that gave almost no warning had ripped through Gaylord. Two people had died as a result. His heart raced with the idea of where Carson might have been when the storm hit.

He stopped and cupped his hand to his mouth. "Carson!" he shouted. He listened for a moment but received no reply. He couldn't imagine how long it might be before they were reunited if Carson hadn't made it back to the campsite. About 50 yards ahead, the chaos of fallen wood thinned where the road cut through a meadow. The woods on the eastern side of the road looked more intact, as though the line of the storm had followed closely along the path of the river. When he reached the better stretch of road, he called out again.

"Yeah, Dad, I'm here!" Carson shouted back. His voice was higher pitched than normal. "I'm at the campsite!"

Relief washed through Isaac. "Jesus, thank God," he muttered. "I'm coming!" he shouted. They called back and forth several times over the next ten minutes. After stepping over rogue branches and circumventing puddles, Isaac walked the two-track down into the opening to their campsite.

The mess of blowdown was too much to take in at once. Nearly a dozen trees lay horizontal across the space. The ground was plastered with wet leaves and smaller branches. A red pine some eight feet around in circumference lay across the length of the campsite. Its fall was broken by the truck. Shit.

Isaac's heart sank. The trunk of the tree rested dead center down the middle of the vehicle length-wise. Anyone sitting in the cab would have been killed. The hood was crimped, leaving the grill with what looked like a maniacal smile.

What good fortune had kept his son from taking cover in the cab of the truck? Pulse beating behind his ears, Isaac scanned the site. "Carson?"

After a moment, movement came from under a group of fallen trees lying against a larger tree like a makeshift lean-to shelter. Moving frantically, a soaking-wet Carson lunged for his father, throwing his arms around his ribs and burying his face in his chest. He shivered and held tight.

"I'm here, buddy," Isaac said, barely keeping himself from falling over. His bad leg twinged a bit from the sudden impact. "The worst is behind us." He held Carson close to him, petting the back of his head. "Are you okay? Are you hurt?"

Carson's head shook back and forth under Isaac's palm. He held to his father as though trying to collapse his ribcage.

"You're saying 'No'? You're not okay or that you're not hurt?"

"I'm not...I'm...I'm not hurt," he managed through staccato breaths. Then, as though his words had conjured it, he broke into a fit of uncontrolled sobbing, a storm of his own he'd been holding in.

Gripping it tight to his chest, Isaac kissed the top of Carson's head. "It's okay, buddy. Let that out. You're okay. You're fine. That was a crazy storm, but it's over. I'm here." He held his son. Looking around the decimated campsite, he couldn't begin to imagine what their next move would be. How would they get home? How would they— He took in a long breath and exhaled through his mouth, giving himself a moment to celebrate that they were both alive and uninjured. That was their good fortune. Everything else could slowly be put back in place, even the truck.

When his breathing idled down, Carson explained that about fifteen minutes after Morgan and Carly had dropped him off, the storm started. His first thought had been to bolt for the truck, but before he could get to it, the big tree came down and demolished it. "I just kinda scrambled around for a minute after that. Trees were coming down all around me. Then I saw those..." He pointed to the trees he'd come out from under. "It looked like the safest place to take cover."

"That was good thinking." Isaac imagined Carson sitting in the cab. He couldn't even allow himself to picture that tree coming down. "Man, we got lucky with you not getting in that truck."

Carson pulled back from Isaac's chest and gazed up into his face. "We need to check on Carly and Morgan."

Isaac looked around them again. How could they check on the girls when they needed to be checked on themselves? He shook his head. "No, we gotta think about what we have going on here first, bud. That Morgan is smart. They'll be okay. I don't think their spot got the brunt of the storm like we did." Still surveying the site, he rubbed a finger along his lower lip. It wasn't lost on him that they could be stuck for days. "We need to take an inventory of what we have. We need a plan. That's first."

Carson nodded, though his pensive face suggested his thoughts were elsewhere.

Isaac found his shoes near where he'd put on his waders earlier. They were drenched. He hadn't decided if they were going to wait for help or try to walk out on their own. If they were going to hike, he'd want dry shoes. He tied the laces together and hung them over a branch. With some effort, they were able to pull their duffle bags from the bed of the truck. The clothes they changed into weren't fully dry, but they were drier than what they had on. Isaac was also able to get the tent out of the truck bed. Given the time of day, it was probably best for them to spend one more night. The doors on the truck wouldn't open, but Isaac could still pull their sleeping bags and pillows out through the shattered back passenger window. Nothing was so wet that it couldn't be used for sleeping.

Carson found his bow undamaged, but his quiver of arrows lay crushed under the trunk of a tree. The only arrow he had left he retrieved from his target some 25 feet in the woods.

"At least the bow is okay," Isaac said. "We can replace the arrows."

Carson nodded. "But you really think Carly is okay? I'm really starting to worry."

Isaac smiled sympathetically and set his hand on Carson's shoulder. "I think they're both likely fine. It might be some time before they can pull that pop-up out of there with what these roads will be like, but it truly didn't look bad over in their direction." He put his arm around Carson. "We kinda gotta focus on ourselves right now for the time being. I need you with me." He pulled Carson into an assuring, one-armed hug.

An idea then hit him. "Do you have any battery left on your phone?"

Slipping the phone up from his pocket, Carson nodded. "Not much, but I've kept it in airplane mode since we've been here."

"Good job. Now, I want you to take it up to the road and see if you can get a signal. If you do, call Ashley, let her know what we're dealing with, and then have her or Ben call up to the ranger station." He stopped and thought for a moment. "They can tell them that we are at the dispersed campsite on Chandler Dam Road. If they can't get anyone to pick up, then they should call the State Police post in Gaylord. If they find out anything, they need to give you a call back. If they're going to send in helicopters, I want to know so we can stay put and just—"

Carson looked at his phone. "I have like 15%. I don't think I'm going to be able to do all that."

Isaac nodded resignedly. "Honestly, I doubt you're going to get a signal, but we have to at least try. Walk around in the fields and stuff. Cover some ground. I had a signal a few times when I was out on the river, so it is possible."

Carson nodded. He then started toward the two-track that would take him to the road.

"Hey," Isaac called after him, "maybe just text Ashley this stuff if you get a signal. I think texting would use less battery."

Carson nodded again and then started up the two-track at a jog.

Isaac called out to him one last time, and Carson stopped and turned. "You're okay, though? You're good?"

"I'm good." Carson smiled weakly. "Good enough." He then disappeared around the bend of the two-track.

Isaac's mind went to the next concern. Food. Looking through the shattered windshield, he could see that the grocery bag with their dry goods was thoroughly soaked. Shit, he thought. He imagined the little they had would be waterlogged beyond being edible. Going to the bed of the truck didn't bring any better news. A limb on the dead-fallen tree had come down through the lid of the cooler, pinning it like a blue-bodied beetle inside an oversized insect display case. With no way to lift the tree, they wouldn't be able to get to the food inside. While packing up earlier, it had made sense to put the cooler on top of the cook stove. They wouldn't see that again either until the tree trunk was somehow removed.

"That's a problem," Isaac muttered. He tried to keep his mind from going to the worst outcomes. Sure, getting his truck out at some point, dealing with the insurance, getting something to drive in the meantime...that was all going to be a pain in the ass. As to their immediate safety, they were fine. Neither of them was injured. They weren't lost. And people knew they were out there as well as their location. With it being August, the temperatures were never going to get low enough at night to be dangerous. The rangers were probably already trying to get to people. The only wildcard was the road. How bad would trying to hike really be? If the rest of the roads were anything like what he'd experienced when he'd first climbed out of the river earlier, trekking out could take days.

Then, another thought. Their only source of potable water was pinned inside the cooler. He patted his front pocket and felt the small protrusion of the lighter. He nodded. They at least had a source of fire. If they really needed it, he could go to the river and fish. Legal size or no, he could catch a bunch of brookies and at least have that for food. And if they were desperate, they could drink the river water. He sighed. When he was packing earlier that week, the idea of bringing his portable water filter would have seemed like overkill. "Can never be too prepared," his father used to say. The old man wasn't wrong. His father also used to tell him, "Make no assumptions in a survival situation." Even though he was reticent about it, his father's Vietnam experience had a way of coming out of him from time to time. He'd always been much graver than the fathers of Isaac's friends.

Is that what they were in? A survival situation? Thinking of it, he went back and looked through the truck's windshield. On the drive up, he'd been drinking from a bottle of water he'd picked up at a gas station in West Branch. Reaching down through a space in the splintered glass, he got his hand to the console cup holder and retrieved the bottle. If the trunk of the tree had made an inch more of progress slicing down through the truck, it would have crushed the water bottle in place. Isaac held it up and examined its half-full contents. A small victory in what was turning out to be a trainwreck of a day.

Even though he'd been trying to push the image of it away, his mind kept going to it. What had that baby stroller been doing in the middle of the river? How did it get there? The story behind it was likely much more than he wanted to know. Or maybe not. Maybe some bored hikers had simply tossed the stroller in the river as a goof. When the storm had stopped, and Isaac had emerged from his cover in the tag alder, the stroller was gone. Likely, it had been washed farther downstream. When the time was right, he'd have to mention it to Ranger Strang. Something about it was troubling, but it wasn't the time to worry about it.

It didn't take Isaac longer than ten minutes to set the tent up again. Unrolling them so they'd dry a little more, he tossed the sleeping bags inside the tent.

Groping his arm into the cab of the truck again, he pulled up what he could of the food in the saturated grocery bag. The remaining cookies were soggy and bloated to twice their size with rainwater. A sealed sleeve of round crackers had survived. He set that aside with the bottled water. After some more rummaging, he came up with three Granny Smith apples, two breakfast bars, and the last quarter of a rolled-up bag of potato chips. Good tight roll, so the chips were dry. He nodded at the haul. It was at least something, enough calories to get them through a day of hiking, maybe two. He had assumed the dry goods were a loss.

His dad was right again. Never assume.

Returning to the bed of the truck, he spotted his utensil box, jammed in place under thick branches, about as inaccessible as the cooler. Among other things, it held their one cooking pot. After a minute of pacing, an idea came to him. He kneeled to one of the back tires and used his buck knife to pry the center cap from the hub. No holes, so if he could get a fire started, he could boil river water in the makeshift chrome pot. He looked toward the tree branch where they'd hung their plastic grocery bag for garbage. By some miracle, it was still hanging in place from its knot. He hunted through it and found three of Carson's plastic pop bottles with their caps still on. Not perfect canteens, but they would do.

He looked toward the two-track. No sign of Carson returning. Maybe he was getting through to someone on the phone. Likely not. It was a time to trust in hope but not get overly hopeful. Optimism would stifle preparation. Still in waders, Isaac started down the path to the river. Here and there he stepped over a fallen trunk, but the predominance of tag alder had largely choked out other trees from growing very large along the water's edge. He shook off a chill. Ever since the storm, the temperature had dropped at least ten degrees. The river flowed dark with stirred up silt. It was rising too as the adjacent wet land and marshes drained off the water they'd accumulated in the storm. Wouldn't be able to fish it with flies at least until the next afternoon, maybe longer. Their rations likely wouldn't be supplemented with fish after all. He filled the pop bottles and then the chrome center cap.

Back in the campsite, he set the water containers down and went to the trees to see if he could snap off at least a few partially dry twigs and thin branches. He hoped he had enough old receipts and business cards in his wallet to get a fire started. Glancing again at his collapsed truck, he sighed. One thing at a time, he reminded himself. He started to examine the branches scattered around the site. Many had been dead, just waiting for nature to give them a good pruning. Though they had a dark sheen of water on their surface, the insides were mostly dry. He climbed up on the hood of the truck and reached into the cab again. Still able to access the glovebox, he found insurance and registration papers along with some other scraps. The important papers could be replaced. His goal was a fire for boiling river water, but also a fire for the night. If the temperatures kept dropping, it was going to get uncomfortably chilly, especially with the damp of everything.

Before trying to start the fire, he cleaned out the fire pit. Then, he gathered up larger limbs and placed them around the perimeter. If he got one started, the flames would help to dry out the bigger logs. Combing over the campsite space, he found larger dead limbs that were also dry on the inside. If he could get initial flames going, additional fuel for the fire wouldn't be an issue. Leaning kindling into a teepee shape in the middle of the pit, he then slid receipts and other scraps of paper into the conical space. He touched the lighter to the paper and, through a process of feeding in more paper and bigger pieces of wood, had a decent fire going within fifteen minutes. He nodded at the sure feeling of the warmth coming off the flames into his extended palms. He draped their wet clothes and shoes over the logs close to the fire.

Then, he looked toward the two-track. Carson had been gone at least fifty minutes, just enough time for a niggling of worry to creep into Isaac's stomach. He put his hand to his mouth. "Carson!" Then, he listened. No response. He decided he'd first set some water to a boil. Then he'd go look for him. Kid was probably being overzealous with his attempt to get a signal. Or worse, he was looking for paths he might use to get to Carly.

Prying off another center cap, Isaac covered it with a t-shirt and strained water from the first cap into it. Using a stick, he raked together a bed of coals and then set the chrome into the bed. He fed more twigs into the coals around the sides of the makeshift bowl. In short time, bubbles began to appear along the bowl's bottom. They slowly broke free and rose to the top. By the morning, the boiled water would be cooled off, free of bacteria, and ready to drink. It could be poured into the pop bottles and carried with them if they decided to hike. He looked around him.

Shelter. Warmth. Food. Water.

In the short term, they were going to be fine. By this time the following summer, the whole thing would be a distant memory...a "remember that one time" kind of story.

Soon, over the crinkle and snap of the fire, he heard them. Tires. Tires rolling slowly over mud and fallen branches. Isaac looked over his shoulder at the headlights approaching dimly down the two-track. Maybe all his preparation had been for nothing. The vehicle coming through the trees was a sedan, so not likely affiliated with the ranger station. Regardless, a handful of cabins had been grandfathered in upstream of where they were camping. Maybe one of the owners had decided on a little scouting mission to see if they could find anyone stranded by the storm.

Isaac stood up and waved toward the windshield of the approaching car. It was a model of Cadillac some five or six years old. Before it came to a stop, the passenger side back door opened. Carson burst out and started running toward him, pointing back at the car.

"Dad! Dad, it's Emily...and Harper. It's Emily. She's not waking up. They brought her up here. These ladies... She's not—"

"Wait...what?" Isaac said, holding up a hand. His throat tightened, and he had trouble swallowing before speaking again. He investigated Carson's pale, panicked face. "What are you...who's 'they'? Ladies?" He stopped and took a breath. He felt dizzy, even numb. "What is even happening right now?"

The car came to a stop, and the passenger and driver's doors creaked open at the same time. An older woman emerged from each door.

CHAPTER 12

Numb, Isaac sat on a fallen tree trunk. His breaths were shallow. The rush of adrenaline had left a metallic taste in his mouth. He looked across the jumping flames of the fire and into the tent where Emily lay unconscious on top of a sleeping bag. The tent flap was tied back, and through the screen he could see Harper kneeling next to Emily's prone body. Behind her, more in shadow, Carson stood hunched, palms on knees, looking down at his sister anxiously.

Appearing no older than the last time he'd seen her, Theresa sat next to Isaac. She could have been 60 or 80 or anywhere in between. She had probably looked middle-aged even in her thirties. She wore boots peeling their faux leather, faded jeans, and a heavy flannel shirt. As she had when he'd met her in Witiko over a decade ago, she had on fingerless gloves and a winter hat. She held his left hand in both of hers and comfortingly rubbed the top of his wrist.

"What is *she* doing?" Isaac said absently, motioning toward the figure that he knew to be Madame Zara, the medium Gwen had been consulting before she died. He still felt dizzy after the chaos of their arrival with an unresponsive Emily in tow. Everything from the prior ten minutes floated hazy in his memory. He knew he'd carried Emily from the car to the tent and checked her vital signs but couldn't remember doing it. He'd done what he could to try to revive her but only remembered lightly slapping her cheeks. He'd spoken too with Theresa, but that conversation was fading like the details of a dream. He'd gotten angry, raised his voice. What he'd shouted, he couldn't recall.

Beyond the tent, Zara threaded her way through the strip of trees that would soon become the tag alder and marsh that flanked either side of the river. When they'd arrived, he'd only registered a few details of the medium in his rush to tend to his daughter. With nearly white hair, Zara wore a long-sleeved, dark blue dress patterned with yin yang symbols, and her fingers clicked with turquoise rings. Her bohemian ensemble was only thrown off by her white, orthopedic shoes. Isaac watched her climbing over a fallen tree. "It gets pretty thick through there if she's going down to see the river," he said to Theresa. "I don't think I have it in me to go searching for her if she gets lost."

"She's looking for reedmace. Cattails, you'd call them. They are known for warding off evil. She's not sight-seeing." She craned her neck, looking toward the other woman. "Be careful, Zara," she called out.

Madame Zara turned toward them. "I'll be okay. I'm not going far," she said. She then continued slowly toward the river.

"Yeah, cattails will help," Isaac said sarcastically. He pulled his hand from between Theresa's palms and crossed his arms. A rush of emotion surged again. "I still don't understand this. Tell me again why the fuck you didn't just bring her to a hospital?"

Sighing, Theresa rested her hands in her lap. "They can't do anything for her. I told you; this isn't medical. She needs to be with you. She needs to be here."

Isaac stood up. "And you know this, how? You're a goddamn doctor all of a sudden?"

Theresa reached up, took his sleeve, and gently pulled him down until he sat next to her again on the trunk of the fallen tree. "I tried to explain this to you earlier, but you weren't in a place to receive it. I'm not sure that you are now. Anger can be a wall." She looked into his eyes.

He turned away from her world-weary gaze. Then, he felt her palm and the soft of her fingers on his face, turning his eyes back to meet hers. "I don't understand any of this," he said after a moment. "What am I supposed to do with this?"

She smiled wanly. "Emily is in danger again. Something is coming after her, something that has pursued her in the past."

He raised a dismissive hand in the air. "And because, like you said, you've *seen* this."

She nodded vehemently. "Both Zara and I did. We had the same vision in a dream. It was a premonition. Your daughter would have been lost if she'd stayed in that house. We saw the Witness Tree. We each saw separately that we needed to bring Emily to you and then to the tree." She reached and held his hands in each of hers. Her grip was warm. "Zara and I...

we pulled into your driveway at the exact same moment this morning. We knew each other's names without having ever met. We'd had the same dream on the same night. Tandem dreaming is very rare between strangers." She stopped and took a breath. "Emily needs to be within the protection of the tree. You need to be there with her. It's been foretold."

He pulled his hands from hers and raised them in the air imploringly. "Are you serious? You mean that stupid survey marker off Sturgeon Valley Road?"

"You know it?" she asked. Her expression turned hopeful. "You know how to get to it?"

"Yeah. They've got it marked. You had to have driven right past it."

"No, we came into the forest from the south. We were on Lost Cabin Trail for most of it until we hit Chandler Dam. We were using a map that Zara had drawn from her—"

"The Witness Tree?" Isaac massaged his forehead with the tips of three fingers. "It's a piss poor excuse for a tourist trap is what it is."

She shook her head adamantly. "No. It's an eternal red pine. Its spirit is resilience. It is evergreen, never going into winter, nor into death. That tree's roots draw from old, deep earth. Think about what it's survived. Fires, logging, neglect. It's not still standing by accident." She closed her eyes, and her head tilted to the left. "Aasha monetoo." She nodded. "Yes, aasha monetoo. The tree spoke its truth to me."

"In a dream?"

She opened her eyes and looked into his again. "Yes, in a dream. We must get Emily to its protection."

Isaac stood again. He couldn't believe she was talking to him about conversations she had with a tree in a goddamn dream. "She's unconscious," he said, raising his voice. "Plus, the roads are all fucked. How are we supposed to do it?" He shook his head. "We just need to stay put until help comes."

Theresa looked up at him, her face showing her sudden realization. "The storm." She nodded, holding up a waggling index finger. "That too was conjured, I'm sure of it. Likely to keep Emily from ever getting to you or to the tree."

Isaac stared. She had told him earlier that the storm had struck soon after they'd turned their car onto Chandler Dam Road. Waiting it out in the car, they were unscathed but then spent almost an hour and a half pulling aside trees that had fallen across the road in front of them. Behind them, the road had been impassable, knotted as it was with tree trunks twisted around each other. "I'd never been so close to a heart attack," Madame Zara had said. "We had tried our best to dissuade the other girl—Harper—from coming up here with us, but to no avail. Thank goodness for her insistence because we really needed her when it came to dragging those branches from our path."

Theresa snapped her fingers up towards Isaac's face. "Are you with me?"

He nodded dumbly.

She looked at him incredulously. "What is wrong with you? Is any of this so hard for you to believe with what you've been through with your daughter already? With Orphan Island? I mean, whatever was out there, whatever maji-manidoo, it's not finished with her. You either open your eyes to that truth, or you lose her."

He looked into her serious face. Then he looked toward the tent again. Kneeling beside her, Harper had Emily's head resting on her thighs. She gently stroked her sweat-damp hair. "What's happening with her, though?" Isaac asked. "Is she dying?"

Theresa reached for his hand. She gently pulled him down to sitting once again. "I don't believe so. I believe she's in a state of metamorphosis. Or more likely, preparing for a state of metamorphosis. If I'm correct, something is after her body again. I fear that Evelyn Cameron isn't done with her."

"What?" Isaac furrowed his brow. "Evelyn's dead."

"Death is not so permanent a thing for those who practice the ways to avoid it."

He held his head between his hands. "Theresa, would you just—"

"Do you remember when we talked on the phone?" she asked. She set her hand on his shoulder. "It was a few months after everything that had happened on the island?"

Isaac crossed his arms. "Vaguely." It was the last time they'd spoken.

"You told me about everything that had happened on the island...everything with Evelyn. You were able to poison her with the lampricide before she could fully possess Emily's body." She took her hand from Isaac's shoulder and worried it over her other hand. "Although she died, I am of the mind now that maybe some of Evelyn's spirit or essence still lingers inside Emily, maybe just enough. If that is the case, your daughter is in grave danger, especially if something seeks to extract and resurrect that spirit."

The light was failing. Isaac sat in the numbness creeping over him. He closed his eyes and squeezed his forehead in his hand. "I don't even...I mean, why her? Why is my little girl—"

"It's not random." Theresa set her hand over her mouth. She took in a long breath through her nose and then exhaled it. She spoke into her palm. "Those with bodies capable of transference are rare. They are gifted or maybe cursed. That's why you were lured to Orphan Island. Even the ease with which you found and purchased the property, it was all likely planned. All the pieces were being moved by an invisible hand, choreographing your arrival for Emily's 11th birthday. She may have been Evelyn's last chance." She took her hand from her mouth and set it again on Isaac's shoulder. "Even your wife's death..."

He swallowed. "What about it?"

She, for the first time, turned her gaze away from his searching eyes. She spoke towards the woods around them. "You must understand that not all hex-born are like Evelyn. Some never experience their gifts. Others accept the limitations of their gifts, like Zara or myself. Then there are some like Evelyn, and likely her clan, who seek to hone their gifts, even corrupt them. Like the addict with drugs, Evelyn's type craves power to—"

"What does this have to do with Gwen?"

Theresa nodded, acknowledging her rambling. "Your accident, the car accident, I don't think it *was* an accident. That raven coming out of the air and into your windshield, blinding you, taking your wife…" Theresa cleared her throat. "She was too much of a wildcard. Evelyn had to be certain of her success. A mother is a fierce, watchful protector—"

"And just what the hell is a father? Are you saying—"

She turned and put a silencing finger to his face. "I'm sure Evelyn saw your wife as a significant obstacle to her plans. Like everything else, I believe her death was orchestrated."

And how, Isaac wondered, had Evelyn seen *him*? Not as an obstacle, but an asset? A father who would be too indulgent of his own grief to be there for his kids? A man who at one time had never really wanted to be a father—had never really seen himself cut out to be one—given the example he had had in his own father? She saw a man who would be just stupid enough to bring his children to an isolated island. A man just blind enough with liquor to overlook the threats to his daughter. Maybe she saw a man who really wasn't much of a father at all. With just him, the children were more vulnerable. He wasn't fierce. He wasn't watchful. He was a blunderer. She'd chosen to keep him alive so he could drive his children, like cattle, to their slaughter.

"Isaac?" Theresa said. "You need to be here. Now. With us fully. You need—"

Something like a squall whooshed in over their heads in the dusky light, a whorl of darkness shaking the leaves and stirring the air with cold. Isaac's first thought was that it was another sudden storm. Then, the high branches of the trees looming above the tag alder exploded with the guttural croaking of a score of ravens landing in them. Theresa jumped, and Isaac caught her by the arm to keep her from falling backwards off the tree trunk. Carson stooped out of the tent with his hands over his ears. "What is that?" he shouted.

Steadying themselves on their perches, the ravens changed their deep throated gurgling into something that sounded as though they were mimicking the soft murmur of a group of women gossiping. They bent their mumbling beaks toward the marshy land below them. Then, just as suddenly as they'd appeared, they lifted off again into flight, their deep-throated crowing dying off as they flew into the northern distance.

Theresa looked at Isaac. "I suppose you'll explain away the ravens by saying that birds can act strange after a storm."

Isaac raked his fingers through his gritty hair. "I really don't know what to say." Goddamn ravens. He walked over and put his arms around a pacing, sniffling Carson. "How you holding up, bud?"

In response, Carson gripped his arms around Isaac. "I'm scared," he said in between shaky breaths.

Nodding, Isaac kissed the top of his head. "I know, it's scary stuff. But your sister is going to be okay." He looked at Theresa, saying it as much to her as to Carson. "We're going to get out of here." Putting his palms on Carson's shoulders, he gently pushed him back until he was looking into his tear-streaked face. "I need you to do something for me, bud. Can you?"

Carson sniffed in a breath and nodded.

"I need you to find me two branches, about six feet or so long...straight as you can get them." Using his thumb, he unsnapped the button on his knife sheath. He pulled out his buck knife and offered it to Carson. "Take this and cut off any small branches. Try to get those longer branches feeling like broom sticks."

Carson's upper lip buckled in against his top teeth in a smile just barely keeping from trembling. He took the knife and nodded. He started to walk, searching among the fallen branches.

"I'll check on your sister," Isaac said.

Carson shook his head. "Not right now. Harper is changing her."

Isaac felt his eyebrow kink when he looked at his son. "What are you talking—" Then a warm hand settled on his shoulder. He looked down into Theresa's eyes.

"She's menstruating," she said in a near whisper. "Her pad needs to be changed every four hours. She could get an infection if we don't." She smiled sympathetically. "Just let her partner handle it."

Her partner? He mostly just thought of them as two oversized kids. He looked toward the tent in time to see Harper's fingers zipping the outer flap shut.

"She really does love her," Theresa said. "I think she would have thrown herself in front of the car if we'd have tried to bring Emily up here without her."

Isaac nodded absently, half listening. That's when things had really gone sideways out on Orphan Island...just after Emily had started her first period. As much as he tried to push the thoughts away, he knew that there was at least some truth to what Theresa was trying to tell him. What he should do in the face of it, he wasn't sure. Where they were, they at least had shelter, including retreating to the interior of the Cadillac. If they were stuck for days, he could still fish. Maybe Carson could even take something down with his bow. They had a fire that they could easily feed with fallen branches for a week, if not more. They could keep water on the boil to purify for drinking. Both Theresa and Zara seemed to know something about Michigan's flora. It wouldn't be goddamn cattails, but maybe they could forage for something edible.

If Emily truly did need protecting, he couldn't think of a much better place to do it. Staying in the campsite clearing, they could watch the edges of the surrounding trees for anyone approaching. Between the five of them, they could keep a close eye on things.

Isaac nodded. Staying put was their best option. Dream or no dream, trying to take his unconscious daughter all the way to the Witness Tree was out of the question. He looked toward Carson at the edge of the campsite near the trail to the latrine. He was holding a branch nearly exact to the specifications Isaac had requested. Using the buck knife, he whittled off some of the smaller branches. No harm in letting him finish, Isaac thought. The task would keep his mind occupied, and there was every chance that they might still need a litter to carry Emily out.

Theresa crouched near the fire. She fed fresh wood into it. Isaac guessed that she and Zara hadn't brought any food with them. With luck, the river would come down enough overnight that he'd be able to fish by the next day's afternoon. Pacing outside the halo of the flames, he noticed the half-light around them working its way toward dark. With the overcast skies, they maybe had a half hour before it would be difficult to see without a flashlight. Where the hell was Zara? Isaac stepped to the edge of the woods where she had gone in.

"Zara?" he called, trying to sound inquisitive more than frustrated, which was what he felt. The last thing they needed was for her to get lost or fall and sprain an ankle, all in the name of cattails. "Zara!" he tried again, raising his voice.

He scanned into the growing darkness among the trees, made darker by the canopy of branches and leaves overhead. He was about to call out again when he saw something moving towards him. With the dark hue of her dress, she could have been anyone, but her white hair and shoes dimly reflecting the available light gave her away.

Isaac reached up to the brim of his hat and turned on his headlamp. The illumination lit up Zara stumbling toward him through the thin trees, her pale face in stark relief against the darkness circled around her. Her left hand clutched at her throat.

Isaac studied her absent expression. Coils of green tendrils hung from her arms and legs. Were those twigs in her wet hair? He leaned a little closer. "Zara?"

She took two teetering steps to the left and then collapsed.

Isaac rushed forward. Zara lay sprawled with her eyes rolled up into the back of her head. With his own heart racing, he shook her arm. Her dress was soaked through. "Come on," he muttered. He pressed two fingers into her throat to the side of her esophagus and just beneath her jawline. He waited but didn't get a pulse. "Theresa?" he called as calmly as he could. "I need you over here. Soon as you can!"

He moved his fingers, trying for the carotid artery again. His fingertips touched on a mucilaginous lump. Jerking his hand back, he saw it in the glow of his head lamp. Attached to her neck just beneath her ear lobe, a jet-black leech squirmed its tail as it fed, like some kind of bonsai sea lamprey. He pinched it between thumb and finger and pulled until its sucking gave way. It left a smear of blood on her pale skin. He tossed it to the ground. Theresa's footsteps approached through the leaf litter behind him. Then she kneeled next to him.

"She was coming toward me, and then she just dropped like a sack of wrenches," Isaac said. "She must have fallen and couldn't get up for a time. She had a leech on her." He cleared his throat. "I couldn't find a pulse."

Theresa sat up from leaning her cheek down to Zara's mouth and nose. "She's not breathing," she said. Her own fingers searched the neck for a heartbeat. "Look," she said, pointing to the green tangle on Zara's sleeve. "This bittersweet and creeper are wrapped tight around her arms and legs." She started for the topmost button on Zara's dress. "She may have fallen, but something clearly kept her from getting up." She unbuttoned a few buttons. "I need to try CPR."

Isaac turned his head back toward the campsite. Carson was sitting on a fallen log, whittling. Thank God he doesn't know what's going on here, Isaac thought. The kid's been through enough for one day.

"Isaac," Theresa said, "I need the light."

He turned his headlamp back to Zara's prone body. Her skin shone like black licorice under the light. "Jesus Christ!" Isaac said.

Theresa gasped and then collapsed into him.

Instead of exposed skin, Zara's open dress revealed her shoulders and chest squirming with hundreds of bloated, feeding leeches.

CHAPTER 13

I tchy-eyed, Isaac leaned forward and fed three thick branches into the fire before sitting back again. A few embers popped outside of the fire pit ring and smoldered on the dirt. Every snapped twig or skittering through the leaf litter behind him had Isaac turning and shining his headlamp into the woods. His lower back ached from sitting on the fallen tree. He had climbed out of the backseat of the Cadillac sometime around what he guessed was midnight when Theresa had woken him for his shift of keeping watch. His sleep had been patchy at best. He looked up at the charcoal sky, guessing that it was close to three o'clock in the morning, though he couldn't be sure. Their phones had all died. When they had tried to turn it over, the Cadillac's battery was dead too. He figured he'd have some idea of the time when the sky began to lighten in the east. The sun would begin to rise around six o'clock, he knew that much.

His hiking boots had dried out after several hours of leaning against a log within the ring of heat emanating from the fire. He had finally been able to change out of his waders. It was a meager blessing in a night that had offered few.

They'd hidden Zara's tragedy from the kids by telling them that she'd decided to go for help. "She's got a friend who has a cabin upstream of here," Isaac had said. "She'll come back and get us if the cabin looks like a safe place to stay until help comes." Outside of Harper wondering aloud if Zara should have gone alone, the two of them largely took the news in stride. Staying loyally by her side, Harper tended to Emily. Carson finished what turned out to be two perfect poles for what would be their makeshift stretcher.

In truth, Zara wasn't going anywhere. Isaac shivered at the memory of it. Recovering from her shock, Theresa had attempted CPR. She pinched Zara's nose closed, tilted her head, and then pushed with her thumb on her chin until Zara's mouth opened. Isaac's headlamp lit up the twitching cavity. He had to look away. Zara's tongue and the insides of her cheeks were coated in writhing leeches. Farther back, under her uvula, the ink-black parasites had her throat choked closed.

Grimacing at the memory of it, Isaac looked again toward the tree line where, some 25 feet beyond it, Zara's body lay. He remembered from a biology course he'd taken that leeches not only secrete an anesthetic to keep their host from noticing them attaching, but they also released an anticoagulant to keep their source of blood from clotting. It was uncertain if she'd bled to death or choked to death or a combination of both.

"Emily's not safe here," Theresa had said, standing up from Zara's body. "None of us are safe here." She shook her head, and her voice cracked. "Poor Zara." She looked up into

Isaac's face. "You're a fool if you don't get your daughter to the protection of the Witness Tree."

He hadn't responded at the time but, sitting in the darkness keeping watch, he knew that he needed to listen. He had to trust that she was right. He had nothing else to trust. He looked beyond the light of the fire to the silhouette of the Cadillac where Theresa slept. Then he turned to the tent where the polyester reflected the flickering light of the fire. Two of his kids were in there. He needed to save them. He needed to save all of them. He stared at the tent, his mind too overwhelmed to really think anything, until he felt the tears sliding over his cheeks. He covered his face with his hands. His eyes burned with exhaustion. Reaching his fingertips up under his glasses, he massaged his itchy eyelids. What was he supposed to do with any of this?

A branch snapped in the woods.

Adjusting his glasses back in place, Isaac stood and looked into the trees where a mist coming off the marsh carpeted the forest floor.

Another branch snapped. Then a shadow moved.

A cold breeze slithered over the back of Isaac's neck. Shivering, he took a few steps forward, not wanting his headlamp to accidentally light up the tent or the inside of the Cadillac. He wasn't going to rouse everybody over what would likely turn out to be a deer.

Another branch snapped. The sounds were getting closer to him. Breath quickening, he reached up and pressed the switch on his headlamp. The illumination lit the tree trunks a dull gray, and among them stood a man looking down at Zara's body.

A fisherman? "Hey," Isaac said after a gasped breath.

The man's pale face turned towards him. A breathy moan escaped his lips.

Isaac took a step back. It couldn't be. It couldn't.

Adam?

He hadn't touched an edible since the first night. His mind was as clear as it could be given his lack of sleep. Tinnitus rang in both of his ears in a high-pitched cacophony. He studied his brother standing in front of him as though he hadn't died over a decade ago. "What are you...?" He took a step forward. It couldn't be his brother. Not alive. Could it be his ghost? At one time, even thinking it would have made Isaac chuckle. Anymore, it not only seemed possible, but probable. He cleared his throat. "Why...why are you here? What do you want?"

Adam turned fully toward him. His pale face was drained of all color. His arms hung limply at his side. He tilted his head.

A car door opened. Isaac stayed with his eyes trained on his brother. His tinnitus stopped abruptly. Then, in the sudden silence of his mind, he heard Adam's clear voice: *I forgive you.*

"Isaac, what are you doing?" Theresa's question was spoken in a hissed whisper.

Isaac looked toward her standing in the space between the open car door and the car itself. He pointed. "My brother," he said, tears breaking from his eyes. "He forgives me for what happened. He forgives me."

She looked at Adam and then looked back to Isaac. "I see him, too. I do," she said, "but you can't trust your eyes. What we are against, they are deceivers. They manipulate and misdirect. Anything could be a trap."

Why would you listen to her? I'm your brother. Do you even really know her, Isaac?

"No," Isaac said. He turned away from Theresa toward his brother who stood with his arms extended, offering an embrace. "Adam," Isaac said. "I'm so sorry." Tears slipped down over his cheeks.

Adam beckoned with his fingers as he had in life when compelling a hug out of a reluctant Isaac. He'd always been the more affectionate of the two. His gray lips rose into a playful grin. *I said I forgive you.*

Isaac knew that smile. He started to take a step. A hand grabbed his arm, stopping him cold. He glared down into Theresa's frantic face.

"You can't," she said.

Just one last hug, Isaac, before I say goodbye.

"Let me go," Isaac said. He wrenched his arm, but Theresa clung like a burr.

"You are not yourself," she said. She pointed at Adam. "That's not your brother. Maji-manidoowaadizi. It's evil..."

I am your brother. Surely you can see that. Why are you listening to her?

Isaac looked at the thin hand holding his upper arm. He peeled the fingers from him. "Get off," he said, pushing Theresa away. She stumbled and fell to the ground. Seeing her clutch her wrist, he winced. "I'm sorry, I didn't mean to, but that's my brother, for God's sake. He wouldn't hurt me."

I'd never hurt you.

"God has nothing to do with him," Theresa said.

Another moan hummed in Adam's throat.

I don't have much longer. His voice sounded fading in Isaac's mind.

Isaac turned away from Theresa and started resolutely toward Adam's extended arms. A cold determination washed through him, and he resolved to not be delayed again from his brother's welcoming embrace. He'd strike her if Theresa tried to stop him again.

Yes. Yes, brother.

Theresa shrieked. "Don't!"

Then, a snap sounded before something whistled past Isaac's ear followed by the sound of pierced bone. In front of him, Adam stood for a moment with an arrow sticking from his forehead before crumpling over backwards onto the ground with a thud.

Isaac stood stunned, staring at the spotlit space where his brother had been. He then turned and looked at Carson standing behind him, bow in hand. Carson shielded his eyes. Isaac's mind felt released, somehow his own again. His tinnitus returned, though much diminished.

"Dad, that wasn't Uncle Adam, goddamnit! It wasn't. Why don't you ever listen?" Tears streamed from his eyes. Carson pointed toward Theresa. "She was trying to tell you..." He dropped the bow and fell to his knees, burying his face in his hands. "Why can't you see? It wasn't him. It wasn't..."

Isaac went to his son and kneeled by his side. He put his arms around him. "I'm sorry. It's okay." He held him tighter. "It's okay." He stroked the back of his head with his palm.

"It's not okay," Carson muttered. "You're not okay."

"He's right," Theresa said, stepping closer to them. "That may have resembled your brother, but I believe it was a golem made, in part, from his remains. I've never seen...I mean, if that's the case, we could be dealing with very powerful magic, maybe even a necroman—"

"Theresa!" Isaac said, shooting her a look over his shoulder. "Don't talk about that right n—"

Startling Isaac, Carson pushed himself from his arms violently. He fell onto his backside. "What, Dad? What? Do you think you're protecting me from something? Do you think I really don't remember, like I somehow forgot everything that happened?"

Isaac stared at his son. He swallowed, and the saliva seemed to catch along his throat. What was he—?

"Jesus Christ, I remember, okay? I still see Silas in my fucking dreams. I can picture his head lying on the ground from you cutting it off with a— I heard the spirits in the lake. I heard..." He dragged his fingertips across his cheek, wiping away a residual tear. He got up on his knees, as though before his father in prayer. "Those girls, the orphan girls, their voices were in my head for days. They wouldn't leave me alone. They told me I had to kill Evelyn before she killed Emily. I was five years old. They told me not to tell you. They told me you wouldn't believe me, wouldn't listen. And you're still not listening!"

Isaac crawled forward and pulled his son back into an embrace. "I know. I'm sorry. I know. I need to listen."

Carson talked into the shoulder of Isaac's shirt. His words came broken and muffled. "I...I could hear him...I could hear whatever that thing..." He shook his head. "It woke me up. He said he forgave you. He said he wouldn't hurt you." He pulled his head back and looked into Isaac's eyes. "It wasn't Uncle Adam's voice, though. It wasn't him. In my head, it sounded like a demon or something..." He collapsed again, sobbing into Isaac's chest.

Isaac looked up at Theresa hovering over them. He locked eyes with her. "We'll take her to the Witness Tree. We will," he said, nodding. "We'll leave at first light. It's not safe here."

Theresa looked at him solemnly. They stayed for a moment in the silence punctuated by Carson's arhythmic, slowing breaths. The cloud cover had broken up, and the full moon shown in the west. Somewhere in the nearby woods, a whippoorwill started its rhythmic, chant-like call:

Whip. Poor. Will. Whip. Poor. Will.

Isaac listened to the bird, a harbinger of the day's beginning. It would be dawn soon. He leaned back and took Carson's shoulders in his hands. "Okay, bud," he said, "we need to start getting ready. I'm listening now. I am. We need to get your sister out of here. We all need to get out of here." He explained that he wanted Carson to take one of the sleeping bags and cut a hole in each of the corners of the foot end. Then, he could slide the poles in along the interior sides of the bag and through the holes. The tip of the buck knife could then be used to puncture some grommet holes through the top and bottom of the sleeping bag alongside the poles. Pushing cut up pieces of fly line through the holes, Carson could tie the poles in place.

"What can I do, Mr. Fletcher?"

Holding his hand over his startled heart, Isaac turned toward Harper with her head poking out of the flap to the tent. Her sleep-matted hair stuck up around her head. He remembered she was wearing a backpack with what he knew to be a Hello Kitty displayed on it. "Okay, I need you to gather up our food and anything else essential that you can find. We'll take what we can, but we want to travel light."

"Okay." She nodded and then her head disappeared. "Let me know before we're leaving." Her disembodied voice came from inside the tent. "I'll change Emily again just before we do."

When Harper came out of the tent to gather the food, Isaac went in. He kneeled at Emily's side, holding her warm hand in his. Her breathing was calm and, more than anything, she looked as though she were having a good sleep. He reached up and stroked away the stray hairs on her forehead. It was cold comfort, but nothing about her suggested that she was in distress. A tear broke from his eye, and he brushed it away. "I'm going to get you out of here, Em. I promise."

Harper pulled back the flap of the tent. She ducked inside. "She's going to be okay, right Mr. Fletcher? She'll be okay?" Her voice cracked on the last word.

Isaac glanced up at her. Her face looked as though she could be a frightened six-year-old. Knees popping, he rose to his feet and put an arm lightly around her trembling shoulders.

"Is this okay?" He recalled Emily saying something about how Harper could be sensitive to someone touching her.

Harper nodded. "It's okay."

"She's going to be fine," he said, assuring himself as much as her. He gripped her a little more tightly. "Do your folks even know you're up here?"

She shrugged. "They probably don't really care one way or the other."

He nodded. "I'm sorry," he said, grimacing. "When we get back, if you want, we can talk about you moving in with us. I mean, if that's something you'd still want to do."

"It wouldn't be forever," she said. "We really just want our own apartment. We need a security deposit, and some places require first and last month's rent, too. We just figured we could save a little living for free at your place. Just for a bit."

"That's a good plan," he said. He wasn't confident that they'd ever come up with the money they needed, but he didn't care. If they ended up living with him indefinitely, then so be it. He gave Harper a small squeeze before taking his arm from her. Glancing down at Emily one more time, he then left the tent.

"Isaac," Theresa said in a hissed whisper. She guided him back into the perimeter of trees that encircled the campsite. Just to the right of Zara's body was a mound of crumbling clay soil flecked with small pieces of white. An arrow stuck out of the mound. "That wasn't your brother, but enough of him to take his likeness." She motioned towards the white flecks.

Bending to the clay, Isaac worked his fingers into the coldness of it. He came up with what looked to be a toe bone.

He slipped it into his pocket and then grabbed the arrow. He stood. A leech wiggled at the corner of Zara's mouth. Next to him, Theresa quietly wept.

"Poor Zara," she said, sniffling. "That's not a way anyone should die."

Isaac put his arm around her as they stood over the body. "We'll cover her before we leave," he said. He leaned down and kissed the top of Theresa's musty winter hat. "And I'm sorry I didn't listen to you."

"It's understandable," she said, after a moment. "We can't always hear what we need to hear." She patted his back before leaning out of his embrace. "We must protect our minds. So much of what we're up against is an endless sleight of hand. Are we leading or being lead? That's always a lingering question to consider."

He thought of the ways Evelyn had likely lured them to Orphan Island. How had Gwen seen an advertisement for the sale of the cabin on Facebook in November when the owners really didn't plan to list it until after the New Year? Had it really been his idea to celebrate Emily's birthday on the island, or had that thought been conjured into his mind as well? What if someone had planted the idea for this fly-fishing trip in his head so that Emily would be alone at the house? What would have happened in his home had Theresa and Zara not taken Emily from it? He didn't allow himself to imagine it.

When he turned his headlamp toward it, he saw where the mound of clay had largely dissolved into the earth. Any trace of bones was gone. He patted his pocket and could feel that the one bone he'd exhumed was still there.

"I need to encourage her spirit along on its journey," Theresa said, gesturing her open palm over Zara's body. "I'm going to stay with her a moment. I won't be long."

Nodding, Isaac started back into the campsite. He heard the beginning of Theresa's chanted song: "G'naadamoimin ina Gizhemanido?" Before anything, he sat on the trunk of the fallen tree. He took deep breaths and then exhaled slowly. It was a technique Gwen had shown him for lowering his blood pressure. Closing his eyes, he shook his head in disbelief. He'd seen his brother standing in front of him, beckoning him. His dead brother. He'd heard his voice. He'd been as real as if he'd truly been there.

Finished with encouraging Zara's spirit, Theresa stepped out of the woods towards the Cadillac.

Taking the small bone from his pocket, Isaac turned it in front of his face. If it were a toe bone, at some point it had been pinched in Isaac's childhood grip. He'd been a doting older brother when Adam was a toddler. As a piggy, the bone had either stayed home or had roast beef or had none. It was too small to be the big toe and too big to be the pinky. He could picture his brother's cherub face beaming at the sing-song game. The "wee wee wee" and fingers tickled up his ribs always set him to laughing.

"All the way home, brother," Isaac whispered. He wiped at the tears streaking his cheeks. He looked around again at the campsite. Carson worked at tying the poles into their stretcher. Harper gathered supplies into her backpack. And, inside the tent, his precious girl lay. Isaac nodded. "All the way home."

After a moment, he stood. He took the water that had cooled overnight and poured it into their bottles. He looked up at the sky and the full moon glowing out of it. Studying it, he nibbled his lower lip. The moon hadn't moved. He listened for a moment, hoping for it, but not hearing it.

The whippoorwill had gone silent.

Out of Carson and Harper's earshot, Isaac went to Theresa where she sat on the hood of the Cadillac, fussing with tying the laces tighter on her boots. "Hey," he said, "I don't think it's getting lighter out, like dawn doesn't seem to be breaking. Or maybe the night's not as far along as I thought."

Theresa finished a double knot on her left boot and then looked up. "Your first instinct—to wonder if something is holding off the light—is likely closer to the truth. Lean on that instinct. It could save you." She turned her concerned gaze on him. "Like I said, we are dealing with powerful conjury. Even slowing or speeding up time to—"

"Just a second," Isaac said, holding up a finger. "Listen." He craned his neck toward the trees on the east side of the campsite. Were those flashes of light?

"Dad, do you hear that?" Carson asked.

"Yeah, but just be still for a second."

The steady murmur of two men talking came from the nearby road. Most of what they said was indiscernible save for a word or two coming through clearly. Then: "Someone's got a fire going over there," a young man's voice said.

Flashlight broke through the woods sending a staggered show of light and dark through the tree trunks. "Is anyone there?" the young man called.

Harper came out of the tent and looked toward the kaleidoscope of light moving about in the trees.

"Yeah," Isaac said, "we're here!"

"We're going to take the road to get to you," a man's voice called. "Give us a minute. We're with the ranger's station. Is anybody with you injured?"

Isaac recognized the voice as belonging to Dietrick who they'd spoken with when they'd arrived at the ranger's station earlier in the week. Isaac cupped his hand to his mouth. "Not hurt, no. Not exactly." He watched their lights, trained on the road, show here and there through the trees. They looked as though they were moving at a jog.

Theresa hovered close by Isaac. "We still need to be cautious."

Isaac looked at her and offered a sympathetic smile. "I have a good feeling about this. It's actual help, I think."

The flashlights turned from the road onto the two-track, sending columns of light through the tree trunks as the two men walked behind it, sweeping luminescence across their path. Each light then flicked off as they neared the glow coming from the fire. It took a moment for Isaac's eyes to adjust. Soon he saw the white of Dietrick Cross' ponytail swinging back and forth from shoulder to shoulder behind him.

"Are you folks okay?"

Isaac motioned toward the silhouette of his demolished truck sitting in the nearby darkness. "You can see what we're dealing with."

Looking at the vehicle, Dietrick gave a sympathetic whistle. "You certainly received the lion's share of the damage," he said. He offered his hand. "I'm sure you remember me. This," he said, gesturing toward the tall, curly-haired young man next to him, "is Luke, one of our summer interns."

Isaac took his hand back from Dietrick's grip. He then shook Luke's hand before calling Harper over for a round of quick introductions.

"Did you see anyone else?" Carson asked. "Were you anywhere near Town Corner Lake?"

Isaac put his hand on Carson's shoulder. "Bud…"

"We were at Town Corner," Dietrick said, nodding. "We were replacing some campsite marker posts before the storm hit." He crossed his arms and shook his head as though someone had asked him a question. "There was nobody in the campground while we were there."

"Not a pop-up?" Carson asked.

"There was a pop-up," Dietrick said, "but no car. No activity as far as I could tell. Did you see anyone, Luke?"

Luke shook his head. "Not me."

Isaac squeezed his son's shoulder. "That's probably good, Carson. Probably after dropping you off they ran into town for something. Maybe they missed the storm altogether."

Carson nodded. "I hope so."

They gathered around the fire to ward off the early morning chill. Dietrick explained that the Town Corner Lake campground wasn't too badly damaged, but the roads out of it were impassable. "Lots of trees down," he said. "We were only able to cut our way through an eighth mile of road before the chainsaw ran out of gas. We had to abandon the truck."

J.C. Vande Zande

The others listened with as much attention as their troubled minds would allow. After a moment, Isaac pulled Dietrick off to the side and explained their situation.

"The girl is unconscious?" Dietrick asked. He held his hand around his chin.

Isaac nodded. "But her vitals are good, and we built a stretcher of sorts for carrying her out of here." He cleared his throat. "She's prone to seizures. The storm triggered a bad one," he lied. "She's been in and out, but we're trying now to just let her rest as long as possible. It takes her a bit to get her strength back. Even when she's conscious, which might not be any time soon, she's not up for any kind of walking."

Dietrick reached his hands behind his head and tightened his ponytail band. Then he tapped a finger thoughtfully against his cheek. "We can take shifts with the stretcher," he offered. "Luke and I can take the first shift."

"We have one more situation, too." Isaac led Dietrick into the stand of trees where Zara's body lay. He told the ranger that she'd gone down to look at the river. He didn't mention the cattails. "We were busy with recovery after the storm. We found her lying here." He explained what they'd found when they opened her dress to attempt CPR.

Dietrick crouched. He opened her mouth and investigated the vortex of black wriggling parasites in her throat. "I've never seen anything like that," he said. He closed the mouth again. Rising to his feet, he pulled his phone from his pocket. "Strange," he said after a moment. "It's out of battery." He scratched his cheek. "Luke? Bring me your phone."

"I will, but it's dead."

Isaac exhaled. "Same thing with all our phones. Could be the storm," he said, but knew that it wasn't. At least he suspected that it wasn't. Still, he couldn't very easily tell Dietrick what he did suspect. He'd sound like a lunatic.

"The medical examiner would probably want some pictures, but..." He looked at Isaac. "If we could, I'd like to use the tent to put the body in. That might provide a buffer for a day or two to keep wildlife away."

Isaac nodded. "Feel free. I didn't plan to take the tent." He raised his eyebrows and motioned his fingers over Zara's corpse. "Only Theresa and I know about this. I'd like to keep it from the kids."

"Of course. That's a heaviness they don't need to carry," Dietrick said, nodding. He called to Luke.

"Please tell him not to say anything," Isaac said, nodding toward Luke's approach.

"Of course."

The intern joined Dietrick and Isaac in the woods. "What are we...oh, shit!" He turned his gaze away from the body. "What the hell happened to her?"

"Be professional," Dietrick said. "You don't have to look, but we need to get a few things for a report."

Dietrick dictated some of the scene's details, and Luke, with his back turned to Zara's body, took notes on a small pad of paper. Isaac went back and, with Carson's help, took Emily from the tent and placed her onto the litter. Harper watched them closely.

"What's happening over there?" Harper asked, motioning with her chin towards Luke and Dietrick's flashlights pointed toward the ground.

Isaac looked over his shoulder and then back to Harper. He shrugged. "Don't know. They said something about finding mushrooms that might be edible."

"In August?"

He shrugged again. "Let's give this a try," he said to Carson, hurrying to change the subject. They picked up the handles of the litter. Emily's body rose with the rising sleeping bag. They hefted her weight a few times. "That's going to work," Isaac said. "Nice job with the poles."

Carson shrugged a humble shoulder.

"Careful," Harper said as she watched them set the litter down.

A whippoorwill began its morning song somewhere off in the trees. Dietrick and Luke walked back to the group. Luke looked as though he might be sick to his stomach.

"Do you really think Morgan and Carly are okay, Dad?" Carson asked. He wrinkled his nose and sniffed in a breath.

Isaac started to answer, but Theresa interrupted.

"I feel that they are both okay," she said. "I think that we are going to see them soon. I can feel it."

Carson looked at her. He nodded. "Okay," he said, looking less distressed.

Isaac glanced to his left at her. Well played, Theresa, he thought.

In the east, the rising sun was slowly washing a lightening gray into the overcast sky.

CHAPTER 14

In the morning light, they stood on Chandler Dam Road looking out over a tree-freckled field to the east. The road was pocked with mud puddles and peppered with leaves and small branches. Above one of the puddles, Emily lay on the litter like a suspension bridge between the towers of Dietrick and Luke. They found a dry spot in the road and slowly lowered her to the ground under Harper's watchful eye. Theresa had wandered off from the group a short distance. Stooped over, she shuffled her fingers through plants growing at the roadside. Carson stood close to Isaac, holding his bow and the one arrow. Hanging from her shoulders, Harper's pink and white backpack stood out in stark relief against the gray skies and storm-wrecked landscape. The backpack's Hello Kitty face was entirely too whimsical for the mood of the morning. Harper stood close to the stretcher looking in the direction Dietrick was pointing.

"Less than a half mile across this field and into those trees, we'll come across the High Country Pathway," Dietrick said. "When we were in radio contact with Nate, one of our other interns, he said Tin Shanty Bridge and Sturgeon Valley roads weren't too bad. The worst of the downed trees were on this road."

Theresa stood up with a fistful of plants with bright blue flowers. "I can confirm that," she said. She pointed to the northwest. "Up around that bend, the road is horrible with fallen trees. I don't think a bulldozer could get through it."

Dietrick nodded. "Given the path of the storm, I don't believe the hiking trail will offer nearly as many obstacles. After this point, the storm seems to have turned west." He then pointed back toward the eastern tree line on the far side of the little meadow. "After about three miles on the hiking trail, we'll come out on Tin Shanty Bridge Road. We can take that to Sturgeon Valley, and from there to Twin Lakes Road and back to the ranger station."

Isaac nodded. The path Dietrick was talking them through would take them right past the Witness Tree. He wasn't sure what he would tell Dietrick about his choice to hunker down at the tree with his unconscious daughter. He could worry about that when the time came.

"We will need to keep moving," Dietrick said. "In our last radio contact with Nate, he mentioned that another line of storms could be forming behind that one."

Carson looked up at the sky pensively. "Then let's get going."

"In just a moment," Dietrick said. "Luke and I need to go back down into the campsite and take a few notes...for insurance purposes regarding your father's truck." He looked at Isaac with an expression that seemed to say, "Not a bad cover story, right?"

Isaac remembered that they still needed to move Zara's body into the tent. "I appreciate it, thanks," he said. He nodded knowingly.

Dietrick took a few strides and then looked back. "Luke?"

Luke shook his head and exhaled. "This internship is wack, man. I didn't sign on for anything foul like *that*." After voicing his protest, he followed a disapproving Dietrick down the two-track.

When Harper had asked about Zara earlier as they made ready to leave, Isaac had simply said, "She must have found her friend's cabin. They may come back for us, but we can't afford to wait around to see when that might be." Returning to stroking Emily's hair, Harper had seemed satisfied with this explanation. "We just need to get Emily to the Witness Tree," she'd said, nodding.

While they waited for Dietrick and Luke to return, Carson stepped a few paces down the road. He stood looking to the south. The way his shoulders moved, Isaac could tell that he was quietly weeping. He guessed that he was probably still worried about Carly. Isaac looked around at the others. Harper kneeled at Emily's side, holding and stroking her hand. Theresa was tying green tendrils around the stalks of the blue-flowered plants.

Isaac stepped up and put his arm around Carson's shoulder. "You okay, bud? I'm sure she's fine."

Carson looked up at him with a red, tear-streaked face. He sniffed in a long breath. "I know it wasn't him. I know it wasn't, but it looked so much like him that...I just keep seeing the arrow stuck in his forehead. I just can't...I'm sorry, Dad." He covered his face with his free hand and cried into it. "I'm so sorry."

Isaac put his arms around Carson and held him against his chest. Jesus, of course that would have to be overwhelming. The poor kid. "It wasn't Uncle Adam, bud. It wasn't at all. I saw what was lying there later...it was just clay. Not even a body. You didn't..." He put his hands on Carson's shoulders and pushed him back. "Look at me," Isaac said. "Look, okay?"

Carson took his hand from his face and looked into his father's eyes.

Isaac smiled and nodded. "What you did, bud...what you did was save our asses. Don't apologize for that. Sometimes the things that need to be done, they seem brutal, but they need to be done. You saved us. Who else was going to do anything? Harper? Theresa? I mean, I was gone...useless, like in a trance. Most people wouldn't have had it in them to do what you did. I'm proud of you." He pulled Carson back in against his chest. "You feel what you need to feel. Cry if you need to, but don't apologize. You did nothing wrong."

Carson nodded his head resolutely.

Dietrick and Luke walked up the two-track toward them. "All set," Dietrick called. "If Carson could carry the stretcher with Luke for a bit, I'd like to speak to Mr. Fletcher."

Isaac looked at Carson. "What do you think, bud? Can you handle that?"

Carson blinked a few times before nodding. "Yeah, okay." He handed his bow with the arrow to Isaac.

Carson crouched at the front of the stretcher and Luke at the rear. After a count of three, they lifted Emily. They started across the field toward the tree line. Harper walked at Emily's side, still holding her hand.

"Azure sage," Dietrick said, pointing to the bundle of stems in Theresa's hands. "We've been seeding it in along the roadsides for a few years now. It's an excellent pollinator and great for honeybees." He tilted his head a bit and studied the bundle in her hand. "Do you have plans for that?"

She looked down at the plant and then to Dietrick. "I was going to smudge..." She looked at Isaac a moment and then back to the ranger. "For a harmonious journey." She smiled. "When bringing together strangers in a common cause...in the culture I was raised in—"

"I'll have to ask you to refrain," Dietrick said. "Though I have little problem with handling the plant itself, I do exhibit allergic reactions to sage smoke." He tilted his head and ran his fingers and thumb up and down along the sides of his throat. "Sometimes it's just an irritant, but other times it has caused my throat to start to close. Unpleasant, to say the least."

Theresa looked at the bundle again. She opened her fingers and let it fall to the ground. "I didn't know," she said. She then caught up to the stretcher and walked on the side opposite Harper.

"Thank you," he called after her. Then, he pulled Isaac's sleeve, indicating that he wanted him to linger farther back. They followed the procession, putting some fifteen feet of distance between themselves and the others.

Dietrick rolled his left sleeve. He spoke quietly. "That woman, your friend...her body was gone."

"What? Like something dragged it away?" A chill shook Isaac.

Dietrick finished the sleeve and then started on the other. "I don't understand when or how it could have happened. That's a brave scavenger when you consider how many humans were within 25 feet of the body."

Isaac shrugged. "The only thing I can think is maybe a bear?"

Dietrick shook his head disbelievingly. "Maybe. I guess that's the only explanation. Either way, please let the family know when you have the opportunity that we will do what we can to recover the remains."

"Okay," Isaac said, nodding. The missing body made no sense. He looked at Carson and the other young man holding Emily aloft. He couldn't help but think of pallbearers. He pushed the thought away.

The Witness Tree, he thought. We just need to get to that tree. He didn't know what would happen there, but Theresa had convinced him that they'd be safe once they arrived. "Let's try to double time it, boys," Isaac called to Luke and Carson. "Crossing this field, we're awfully exposed."

Luke looked over his shoulder at him. "Exposed to what?"

Isaac rubbed his forehead. He couldn't very well say that they'd be exposed to animals spying on them. "If more storms come through, you'll know what I mean by exposed," he said.

Luke picked up his pace.

Having crossed the field, they headed into the woods. Most of the trees seemed largely untouched by the previous day's storm. They weaved their way through them. In short time, they found the High Country Pathway running across the surface of the forest floor like a long scar between the trees.

Dietrick pointed to the left. "This way will take us out to Tin Shanty Bridge Road." He looked at Carson and Luke. "Are you two good for a while yet?"

Adjusting their grips on the poles, they nodded.

"Okay, then."

Dietrick led the way, followed by the stretcher, and then Isaac taking up the rear. Under the overcast sky and canopy of branches, they walked in diminished light, something close to dusk. The woods still held the damp of the storm, and the forest gave off the mixed odor of ozone, plant oils, and stirred up bacteria from the soil. Petrichor, Isaac remembered, the name for the distinct smell of the woods after a rain. Though not as bad as the campsite, the trail was not without obstacles. Their progress was slow, but steady. They worked their way around enormous puddles. They stepped over or ducked under fallen branches. A line of trees across their path like a snake of tumbled dominoes sent them deep into the forest until they worked their way around the final crown and could follow the other side of the trees back to the trail.

Other times the trail was generous, and they might walk a quarter mile's length without hindrance. Sweating and thirsty, they stopped to rest in an area of downed trees. After setting Emily down, Carson and Luke shook out their arms. Isaac rationed out some of their food supply. He then passed around water.

Everyone grumbled about their wet feet.

"Next summer, I'm working at Taco Bell like a normal person," Luke said. "This is bullshit."

Dietrick shot him a look.

"What?" Luke said. "I'm not joking."

"Well, we'll take the next shift with the litter," Isaac said. "You boys did good."

"Look," Harper said, smiling. She'd propped Emily up and held a water-soaked rag to her mouth. Even unconscious, she nursed from the wet cloth.

Isaac recalled his mother doing something similar while sleeping through a recovery from chemotherapy. Seemingly dead to the world, she would instinctively suck at the wet sponge they placed to her chapped lips. He watched his daughter behaving nearly the same. "Nice work keeping her hydrated, Harper."

"I suspect we are less than an hour from the road depending on the condition of the rest of the trail," Dietrick said. "If they've already done some clearing, Ranger Strang might be able to pick us up. I'm sure they're patrolling the accessible roads."

Theresa sidled up to Isaac while Dietrick spoke. "Have you seen them," she said, motioning to the trees. "The chickadees have been following us since we started on the trail. They stopped when we stopped." She shook her head. "We aren't alone."

Chewing a cracker, Isaac looked into the surrounding branches at the little black and white birds pivoting their curious heads at them.

"At this rate, even if we end up on foot the whole time, I suspect we can be back to the ranger's station well before dark," Dietrick said.

The chickadees began to trill their three-note song. They circled around the group, flitting from branch to branch, gradually increasing their speed. Then they left the branches altogether and turned in a gyre some three feet above them. Individual birds broke from the circle, dive-bombed close to their faces, and then rejoined the others.

"Get out of here," Luke said. He swatted his hand at one of the little kamikaze birds.

"They're acting as though they're protecting a nest," Dietrick said.

The birds continued their circling while increasing the volume of their song: Chicka dee dee dee dee dee. Chicka dee dee dee dee dee. Chicka dee dee dee dee dee.

Carson circled his arms around his head. "Jesus, shut up, stupid birds."

Dietrick stood. "That's peculiar," he said, still observing the birds. He then stifled a colossal yawn. "Good god," he mumbled. "I'm exhaus..." He staggered a few steps into the woods before crumpling to the ground in what looked like a dead sleep.

Luke dropped face first onto the ground from the tree trunk he'd been sitting on. His snoring was instantaneous.

Chicka dee dee dee dee dee.

"Cover your—" Theresa started. She slumped her full weight into Isaac. Then, she slid down his body and curled into the fetal position on the ground.

Isaac took a step back and leaned his spine into the trunk of a tree near the trail. He turned toward the stretcher, and his eyes took a long, slow-motion blink. When his lids opened again like a stage curtain going up, his vision revealed Harper, out cold, lying side by side with Emily.

"Dad?" Carson managed. "Are you super tire..." He fell to his side and slept. The apple he'd been eating rolled from his grip.

Isaac's body sagged down the tree, leaving him sitting amongst its exposed roots. Sleep washed over him as tangibly as a wave off Lake Superior covers the beach sand. He felt heavy with it, weighted down. His head lolled to the side. "Hey," he said to nobody. He tried to fight it, but his eyelids dropped again, leaving him in a long blackness...

A branch snapped. Isaac's left eyelid drifted open reluctantly. It was dark. Nighttime. In the blue-gray moonlight filtering through the overhead branches, Carson and Luke's bodies were still strewn in front of Isaac's canted vision, lying in the same positions as he'd last seen them. The temperatures had dropped, and a fine mist flowed across the ground. Cold crawled over his skin.

He tried to call out to Carson, but no words came. No tension in the back of his throat. No movement of his jaw or tongue. He felt only the desire to speak and nothing more.

Neither would his eyelid blink. His eye stared straight ahead, fixed in its socket as though glued into place. He could see the young men in his field of vision, but not Emily nor Harper to his left. Not Dietrick in the woods to his right. A tear broke from his duct and slid down his cheek. His eye continued to water.

Though he willed it, nothing on his body moved. His breaths were shallow, barely moving his ribcage.

Another branch snapped, but he couldn't turn his head or flick his eye toward the sound. If his heart was racing, he couldn't feel it. He heard a murmur on the air that sounded like old women gossiping. The murmur soon stopped. A malodorous odor permeated the mist and seeped up into his nostrils, instantly transporting him to the basement of his childhood. About twice a year, his father used to bring Fritz, their Golden Retriever, down to the silver washtub for a bath. He always made Isaac and Adam help with the drying. The smell of wet dog hung on them afterwards until they were finally able to have their own baths.

The same musty smell, though much stronger, hung in the air around his unmoving body.

Down the trail, a tall shadow lurched out from the trees. Its fur-covered body made for a jagged silhouette against the gray light around it. It resembled a wolf standing on its hindlegs except with a crown of antlers between its ears. Its white-tipped tail jutted out straight from its body, echoing the white fur of its throat. It walked rigid and unsteadily, seeming to survey Luke and Carson's bodies in front of it. It turned its long snout toward the moon, and the sound out of its throat started as a howl and ended as a human scream.

Somewhere to the west, a band of coyotes answered, filling the night with an inharmonious jangle of high-pitched warbling.

Isaac's bladder emptied, sending a wash of wet warmth over his crotch.

The creature staggered awkwardly. Its long arms hung down, sometimes touching the ground or the trunk of a tree to help keep itself upright. It walked as though bones had been broken in its body and then healed out of place. It sniffed deeply along Carson's length before stepping over him. It stopped again briefly to smell the apple.

Turning its snout to its right, it stalked out of Isaac's peripheral vision to where Emily and Harper lay. The attempts Isaac made at movement were futile.

The inquisitive sniffing punctuated the otherwise near silent night. The voices of the old women on the air began the communications of their clutch again. Their indiscernible words whispered on the edge of Isaac's earshot.

Before Isaac could go mad with imagining what it might be doing to his daughter, the creature lurched back into his line of sight. The urine on Isaac's skin had started to cool, sending a spasm of shivering up his spine.

The creature twisted its neck abruptly and locked its ice blue eyes on him. It took ratcheting steps forward, as though movement were painful, a low growl percolating in its throat. Its mouth hung open slightly, and moonlight reflected off its fangs.

Isaac felt the same way Emily had often described her panic attacks, frozen and waiting helplessly for an impending threat. He couldn't do anything. He swallowed and the saliva caught along his sleep-slowed throat. Sweat beaded across his forehead and dripped down his back.

The creature approached slowly, dropping down to all fours and crawling toward him. Its eyes stayed locked on his one open eye. Saliva dripped over the edge of its lower lip and drooled in ropey strands to the ground. Maggots crawled in and out of the holes of its rotting antlers. Its wolf-like head sniffed at Isaac's ankle, pressing its way up his calf and then inner thigh. It nosed searchingly into his urine-soaked crotch, pushing its snout, drawing out a pain that would have doubled Isaac over if he could have moved. The creature's glowing gaze looked up into Isaac's watery eye.

Working its way up Isaac's torso, it stopped and inhaled deeply from the skin of his neck. Its breath was humid and cold at the same time. The weight of its presence felt as though it were smothering Isaac. Nearly unconscious with terror, he willed everything he had into closing the lid of his exposed eye. It finally descended just as the creature's salivating, hot breath washed over Isaac's face. Its staccato sniffing probed his forehead, his cheeks, and into his ears. Its rancid fur brushed across his skin. A deep, growing growl emanated from its throat.

Then, with a suddenness, it was gone, leaving a damp cold in its wake and the faintest whispers of the old ladies' voices on the breeze.

After a moment, Isaac forced his eye open again, like a sticky tambor on a rolltop desk. As much as he wanted to stay in the safety of not seeing what was happening, he had to know if his children were safe. His other eye opened too in time to see the creature lifting Luke's body in its arms. It held him face up, and Luke's arms and legs hung limp from his torso as though he'd been lifted down from a cross.

The murmuring of the old ladies faded.

Swiveling its gaze to the woods, the towering canine tilted its neck and howl-screamed a second time. The distant band of coyotes soon answered. The hair on Isaac's neck stood up, tingling. With a final menacing look toward Isaac, the creature hoisted Luke over one of its shoulders and bolted into the dark woods at a galloping three-legged run.

CHAPTER 15

Shivering in the falling temperatures, Isaac surveyed the prone bodies of his children and the others. The night was soundless. He strained to hear anything that might broadcast the return of the nightmarish creature. As the minutes passed, feeling slowly came back to his shoulders and hips and then down his limbs and into his extremities. In time, he pushed himself to standing, steadying himself with an arm against the trunk of the tree behind him. His crotch, wet and cold with urine, ached dully. He checked first on Emily and then Carson. Both lay unmoving, breathing nearly imperceptible breaths. Neither seemed in any kind of distress. Examining Harper and Dietrick, he wouldn't call what they were experiencing sleep so much as hibernation. Using his fingertip, he opened one of Theresa's eyelids. Her eyeball stared straight ahead with all the life of a glass eye. The pupil dilated and contracted sluggishly as the light from Isaac's headlamp passed over it.

He lightly slapped the flat and back of his fingers against Theresa's right and then left cheek. "Theresa? Can you hear me? Blink if you can hear me." He released her eyelid and it drifted shut. It didn't open again. "Come on, I need you here," he whispered. He couldn't imagine what his next move might be if they didn't start coming around soon. If he secured her legs to the litter, he could probably drag Emily to the Witness Tree on his own. Still, he couldn't very well leave the others lying helplessly while that thing was out there. Pacing, he looked at the darkness all around him and then slowly sank down until he kneeled on both knees in the middle of the path. "I don't know what I do here," he said, shaking his head. "What do I do here?" He looked toward the sky as though some solace might be found there.

As though answering his question, the wailing of a baby came out of the eastern darkness of the forest. Isaac rose to his feet and looked in the direction from which the crying had come. Was he hearing things again? A city block or so into the trees, a window's rectangle of yellow candlelight trembled in the darkness. Something inside the cabin limped slowly from one side of the window to the other. Isaac squinted, not certain that what he was seeing was what he was actually seeing. A moment later, the light flickered out.

The baby cried again.

Isaac turned and looked at his children and then at the others on the ground. Not so much as a pinky finger twitched among them. When were they going to come to?

Nothing will happen to them, a woman's comforting voice spoke into Isaac's troubled mind, instantly calming it. He looked again towards where he had briefly seen the window of light in the woods. He felt secure, even buoyant, about everything, the way he remembered feeling in the peak euphoria of an evening's drinking, before adding more drinks would spoil the rest of the night.

Go to the infant. Save it.

Nodding, Isaac reached up and turned on his headlamp. He looked again at the bodies around him in torpor.

I will watch over them.

He nodded again. They would be safe. He was certain of it. Without giving them any further thought, he started into the dark woods, following the path of light his headlamp beamed in front of him. Branches snapped under his footsteps. Cold air washed over his forearms. He rolled down his sleeves. In short time, the squared outline of a log cabin faded into the light. Squat and gray in the halo of luminescence, the cabin couldn't have been much bigger than a one-car garage. A black rectangle loomed where the cabin's entry door used to be.

"Hello?" Isaac called, cupping his hand to the side of his mouth. "Is someone here? Are you okay?" He thought of the stroller. Maybe the parents or at least one of the parents was here with the baby. Maybe they'd been caught by the storm and had taken refuge in the dilapidated cabin. "Hello?"

He was answered by the baby's muffled crying coming from somewhere inside. He swallowed, studying the gaping maw of the canted entrance. The structure leaned to the right, looking as though it might collapse into itself at any moment.

Go in.

Something landed in the branches of a tree above him. It adjusted itself for a moment on its perch and then made no more noise. He turned his light up toward the sounds of its landing but saw nothing.

The baby cried out again in a high-pitched yowl. Isaac recalled the cries of his own children when they were infants. With no words, they had only the one desperate way to express their hunger, tiredness, pain or discomfort.

"Is anybody here with that baby?" Isaac asked, raising his voice. "I don't want to startle you." He felt the exaggerated pumping of his heart in his chest. The backs of his wrists were warm with sweat. He took a long breath and exhaled it slowly. Looking back toward where he knew his children lay, he saw nothing save for the staggered trunks of trees caught in the glow of his headlamp.

They're safe.

Nodding, he set his hand against the left jamb of the cabin's doorway. The damp, cold air from inside the cabin drifted out over the threshold. He shivered. Leaning his head through the cabin's door frame, he swept his light over the inside. Its contents were sparse, including a simple, dust-covered dining table, a chair lying in a heap of its pieces, and a metal bedframe with no mattress. In the corner, a pile of what were likely raccoon bones sat nested inside its dried out, decaying husk of skin and fur. The mantle of a stone fireplace sat opposite him. Its firebox was filled with smaller stones, some of which spilled out onto the floor. The chimney had likely caved in on itself.

Isaac swept his light into the rafters, half expecting to see them dangling with bats, though he knew that at this time of night they would be out hunting for insects. Something with metal rods and pieces of brittle leather hung from one of the rafters. Isaac examined it, and his mind put together the details. It looked to be an antique polio leg brace.

As Isaac lingered in the doorway, what felt like a cold hand shoved him from the back, sending him stumbling into the interior of the cabin.

He barely kept himself from falling and then, standing in the middle of the room, he turned around abruptly with his fist cocked back. Where the doorway had been, his headlamp lit up only more log wall, as though the threshold had never been there. He turned a full circle and found the interior of the cabin to be nothing but walls, not even a single window. A warm drop of sweat broke from his hairline and slid down his back.

He was trapped, cut off from his children. As far as he knew, they still lay nearly catatonic on the forest floor. That creature was out there somewhere. Isaac paced the boundaries of the cabin's interior. After kicking the walls in several places and finding them more solid than he would have guessed, he dropped to his knees in front of the fireplace. He began shoveling stones to the side with his sweating palms. He hoped to find a way to climb out of the cabin by going up what remained of the chimney. It seemed his only choice.

The woman spoke into his mind again: *I told you that they would be safe. You need not worry for them.*

As before with hearing her voice, a sense of security and calm washed through him, not unlike the time he'd had an appendectomy, and they'd treated his initial pain with morphine in his IV. Each administration of the pain killer had left him smiling, intoxicated with joy.

"I still need to get out of here," he said, maybe to her, maybe to himself.

The baby's crying started again, muffled and mewling. It sounded as though it had come from below him. Isaac stood up and paced to the middle of the floor. He listened. After a moment, the baby cried out again, and Isaac was certain that it was coming from beneath the floorboards.

Save the child.

"Wha...how?" He staggered around the space, shining his light over the pine planks. In a corner near the front of the cabin, he spotted a hinge in the flooring. And then another. Not far from them he found the inset cast iron ring handle. Gripping his hand around the cold metal, he pulled open the hatch. A musty smell of decaying vegetables, earth, and sawdust wafted up from the exposed opening. His headlamp revealed the top of a ladder disappearing down into the darkness of a root cellar.

The baby cried again, and he could hear that its cries were less muffled now that he'd opened the hatch. "I'm coming, little one," he called down into the hole. "I'm coming." Stretching a leg down into the cool darkness, he set his foot on a rung of the ladder. Feeling its sturdiness, he lowered his other foot down to the same rung. He stood for a moment with his lower half underground and his upper half above it. Taking a breath, he reached his left foot down, waiting to feel the solid perch of the next rung. He continued his slow descent.

A chorus of murmuring women's voices circled around the outside of the cabin. They gasped and moaned as though they stood on a shore watching helplessly as a beloved child drowned in the middle of a lake. What sounded like fists pounded on the outside walls, shaking the interior. The leg brace fell from the rafter to the floor, clattering into pieces of metal and leather. Standing on the rung, Isaac felt suffocated in dread. Something bad was going to happen. Out of instinct, his right leg lifted toward the next rung up. When it did, the rung still under his left foot cracked in half, sending him plummeting down the hole. The trapdoor slammed shut above him. He took the brunt of the landing on his back, knocking the wind from him. The light from his headlamp flashed wildly around the blurred earthen walls as he struggled to take a full breath.

When he could breathe again, he lay for a moment on the cold ground taking an assessment. Though his back ached from the impact, none of his limbs were broken. Even his bad leg seemed fine considering the distance he'd dropped. He patted his hand around the earthen floor until his fingers touched down on the temple of his glasses. He slid them up onto his nose and over the tops of his ears. He exhaled a sigh, seeing that both lenses were still intact. His clear vision revealed walls of makeshift shelves with withered carrots, potatoes, and cabbage. A few yellowed mason jars held what looked to be canned fruits, vegetables, and preserves. He climbed up to his feet and listened.

Above him, the cabin had gone still. The voices and pounding were silenced.

The baby whimpered from somewhere nearby, sounding exhausted.

Find the infant.

Isaac nodded. Shining his light around the small space, he spotted the entrance to a tunnel in the corner. He kneeled down and shined his light into the blackness. The crown of the tunnel dangled with thin roots. The length of the shaft outlasted the range of his light.

The baby's crying came from the far end of the passageway.

"Jesus Christ," Isaac muttered.

You're running out of time...

"I can't..." Isaac started, but then just shook his head. There was no way the baby was going to come to him. He took a deep breath and started into the entrance. He crawled on hands and knees for about five feet before the narrowing passage pressed him down to his elbows. Not much farther along, he was forced into an army crawl, ratcheting himself forward and pushing with what purchase he could get from his feet, knees, and hips. If he was moving, he could keep himself from getting too consumed in the closing in of the space. He was staying one inch ahead of crippling claustrophobia. The sounds of the baby were growing closer too, motivating him to keep going despite the spikes of panic when he'd try to imagine how he was going to get out. If he was going to get out...

You're almost there.

Isaac kept on, even as the sides of the tunnel squeezed his shoulders. As he inched forward, his sleeves saturated with water that had wicked up into the floor of the tunnel. After struggling his way through a tight spot, he lifted his head. The light from his headlamp revealed something moving.

It wasn't a baby.

Instead, his lamp lit up a sickly coyote staring at him with red eyes. The only way to describe its expression would be to say that it was smirking. The animal was largely furless from mange, and its skin was a mosaic of either crusted over or freshly scratched wounds. It lay at the end of the tunnel in what looked to be a small den. Isaac was wedged at the threshold. Keeping its eyes fixed on him, the coyote rose to standing on three legs. Atrophied to a quarter of its size, its left front leg dangled from the shoulder joint like a twisted stick. Drool dripped over its cracked lips. The air swam with a scent of decaying flesh.

Thought had abandoned Isaac, leaving him to react only out of instinct. His body jerked and shimmied with his desperate attempts to get some kind of backwards movement. As he kicked and scrambled, he felt the crown of the tunnel give way, pinning him from the waist down under collapsed earth. He struggled to take a full breath.

The coyote stalked toward him. Opening its mouth, it emitted a sound just like that of a baby crying in distress. Then it laughed a staccato laugh, sounding first like a woman— whose voice this time brought Isaac no comfort or calm—and then like an old man chortling vindictively. "I'll start with peeling your face from your skull," the coyote spoke in the old man's voice.

While the canine laughed mercilessly, an invisible force picked it up and slammed it against the wall, where it stayed as though it had been hung there on a nail. Its eyes bugged out, and its tongue protruded over its pink, blood-stained teeth. Whatever the unseen entity, it clearly had the coyote by the throat.

A man's voice, confident and ethereal, boomed into the space of the den. "You will leave him be!"

The coyote thrashed against its captor's grip, only to be jerked back from the wall and slammed into it again. It gave a choked-off yelp.

"You're a long way from home, skincripple," the man's voice bellowed.

Isaac watched the coyote slide up along the wall, like an iron filing pulled by an unseen magnet, until it was pinned against the ceiling of the den. Its good legs dangled helplessly, kicking. Its scrawny front leg curled and pressed in against its ribs.

"How long did you think your presence would be tolerated? You're wanted here no more than you were wanted by your own pack, outcast. You may have felt called, but this land does not want you here."

Through its choking, the coyote managed something that sounded like speech. "T'áá hó\'ájitéégóó, t'éiyá."

"I don't understand your tongue. If you're asking for mercy, be gone from this forest before light touches the eastern sky. The faster I forget, the better for you."

"I'll leave...I'll be gone," the animal croaked, still speaking as an aged man.

Isaac watched as the canine suddenly dropped, yelping again as its side slammed into the ground. After a moment of recovery, it scrambled up to stand on three legs. With no acknowledgement of Isaac still wedged in the tunnel, the coyote found its bearings and turned three quick circles, seemingly chasing its own tail.

Everything went black.

Moments later, when Isaac's sight faded in to the half-dark around him, he lay on the forest floor with his lower body under a pile of leaves and sticks. The full moon's light filtered through the leaf canopy overhead. Kicking out from under the debris, he scrambled to his feet. Though he stood where it had been, there was no trace of the cabin. He staggered over to a tree and steadied himself against its sturdy trunk. His settling adrenaline mixed with relief and lingering terror had him feeling as though on the verge of uncontrolled sobbing. "There's no time..." he managed, his voice cracking.

"Dad?" Carson's groggy voice called. "Where are you?"

Isaac hastily brushed the back of his hand under each eye. He sniffed in a long breath. "I'm here, bud! I'm here."

Following his headlamp's light, he started at a jog through the trees back to the others.

CHAPTER 16

Dietrick stood near the edge of the trail looking into the woods. Silver-white ponytail almost glowing against the dark backdrop, he cupped his hand to his mouth and shouted Luke's name. Carson did the same on the other side of the trail. Hunched under the makeshift privacy tent made from one of Isaac's long-sleeve shirts, Harper used the headlamp to take care of Emily's sanitary needs. They had all started to wake up some five minutes after Isaac had come back from the cabin in the trees. Aside from Isaac, they had no knowledge of Luke's abduction.

Under the guise of going down the trail to look for signs of Luke, Isaac and Theresa put their conversation out of earshot. He filled her in on what he had witnessed.

"The man's voice in the den...there's something benevolent here," she said, nodding. "Something here seems on our side." She shivered. "The wolf-creature sounds like a wiindigoo, a shapeshifter, a tortured creature born of cannibalism." She shook her head. "I hold out no hope for Luke." She looked at Isaac knowingly, as though to indicate that the search for the intern was pointless. It served only to delay their crucial arrival to the Witness Tree. "The other thing in the cabin—the sickly coyote— I'd say it was a skinwalker, but I've never heard much of their activity on this side of the Mississippi. The maji-manidoo here must be calling them. Much is in movement."

"Whatever any of it was it was terrifying," Isaac said. He shivered, pushing the experience of it from his mind. He willed himself to stay present, to not get lost in the paralyzing memories of the last hour. He could break down after Emily was safe...after they were all safe. "The question is what do we tell Dietrick, if anything?" he asked.

"Do you think he'd even believe you if you told him the truth?"

He motioned his hand toward the trail behind him. "Considering we all fell asleep like narcoleptics and woke up in the middle of the night, we might be able to cut through his skepticism."

Theresa took his sleeve in her hand. She closed her fingers into a fist. "I'm here to help you get your daughter to the Witness Tree. It's my only purpose. How much time we have, I don't know." She looked over Isaac's shoulder at Dietrick and then back to Isaac. "If we're delayed here looking for that young man—a young man who is likely dead—I can't predict what that will mean for Emily. I don't mean to be cold, but spending any time looking for Luke is a lost cause."

Isaac looked back at Dietrick who continued to call for the intern.

Theresa tugged his sleeve until Isaac looked at her again. "If he believes Luke somehow got lost...well, protocol would likely have him stay at least until daybreak. That won't do." She pulled hard on his sleeve again. "Look at me. You can still save Emily. Everything is telling you what you need to do, but you have to do it."

He stared into her eyes, his mind elsewhere. She was right. There was no explaining the creature or the cabin. And even if Dietrick did believe him, she was probably right about him committing to finding Luke or at least staying where Luke was last seen. They didn't need Dietrick, but it certainly didn't hurt to have an extra person around. Stretcher duty would be challenging without him. Plus, it didn't seem right to leave him there alone with that creature roaming the woods. After a moment, he nodded to Theresa. He was resolved. He turned toward the others. "Hey, Dietrick," he called, "I didn't really want to tell you, but the kid bailed. I was kind of hoping he'd think better of it by now and come back."

Dietrick took a few steps towards Isaac. "What?"

"Yeah, he woke up right after I did. He didn't wander off. He left. He said this internship was bullshit, not what he signed on for. Said he could get out of here twice as fast without us."

"You're serious?" Dietrick studied Isaac for a moment. "He had an attitude, no doubt, but I have a difficult time seeing him abandoning us."

"Well," Isaac started, "I'm not lying—"

"No, I didn't mean to say—"

Isaac held up his palm. "I'm just saying, it's in situations like this that a person's true colors can come out." He stopped his line of argument. He didn't want to besmirch the kid any further. "Look, he was probably just scared. Hell, I'm scared." He crossed his arms. "I don't know how we all passed out in the middle of the day. I don't know what's going on now. I just know we need to get back." He cleared his throat. "Luke left that way down the trail," he said, pointing, "so we're most likely to run into him if we just keep going."

Dietrick moved closer to Isaac. "I really don't understand any of this. The unprecedented storm..." He leaned in closer so only Isaac would hear. "...the woman's body disappearing. Then what happened here," he said, gesturing toward the ground, "with all of us seemingly losing consciousness at the same moment. And now Luke..." He shook his head. "Everything I do to try to explain it to myself ends up sounding quite far-fetched."

Harper came out from under the shirt and began to fold it. "Emily's ready now," she said. "We should go."

Isaac looked resolutely into Dietrick's face. "You can stay here calling for him if you want, but I need to get my daughter out of here."

Dietrick shook his head. "No, if you say that he went down the path, we'll go that way. We need to stay together as much as possible."

The young man was likely dead. At the least, there's nothing much we can do to save him, Isaac thought. Emily could still be saved. As he had with many distressing thoughts, Isaac pushed Luke from his mind. He passed the last of the food and water around. In short time, retrieving it from Harper, Isaac turned on his headlamp and lifted the front of the stretcher. Dietrick lifted the back handles.

Isaac called Carson up to him. "Take up the rear." He leaned in closer and whispered. "Keep your arrow nocked."

Carson gave him a quizzical look but then nodded. He took up the position at the end of the procession. They followed the cone of light coming from Isaac's headlamp. Theresa walked to the side of the stretcher and sang under her breath. "Giin gosha naa. Mi isa wenji-bimoseyaan."

"What language is that, if I may ask?" Dietrick adjusted his grip on the handles. "It's quite moving."

"Ojibwemowin."

"What do the words mean?"

She looked back at him and then set her hand atop one of Emily's hands. "They don't mean so much as are, like with us. The pitch is what's most important." She turned back to face the trail coming out of the darkness into Isaac's light. "If I had to translate, I'm asking the Great Spirit to watch over us as we travel, but even the melody affects the translation." She looked back at Dietrick again. "Sung differently, it's also a song for the dead, smoothing their passing into the next world."

Emily moaned in her unconsciousness.

"Keep singing," Harper said. "If you don't mind. I think she likes it."

Soundtracked by Theresa's hushed singing, they followed the trail northwest. Very few trees were down, and the sticks on the trail weren't very substantial. They were making better time.

"I'm not sure this area was touched by the storm much at all," Dietrick said. "It's a good sign."

"Dad?"

Isaac looked to his right to see Carson walking alongside him. Carson shielded his eyes from the sudden light in his face. Staring ahead into the halo of luminescence from his headlamp had made the darkness at its edges all the blacker to Isaac. "What's up, bud?" he said, turning the brim of his hat again toward the trail.

"There's something following us," Carson said. He looked past Isaac into the darkness of the woods.

"I see them too," Dietrick said. "By the yellow eyeshine, I'd say they're coyotes."

"Hey now!" Theresa shouted. "Scat!" She stamped her feet.

The yellow orbs darted deeper into the woods and then circled back.

"They're usually pretty skittish," Theresa said.

Yeah, *usually*, Isaac thought. He decided to keep his encounter from the other night to himself. "Look, we'll just keep going. We gotta be getting close to the road," he said. "Carson, you keep an eye on them. If they come in closer, we'll set Emily down and circle around her. Theresa and Harper, if you see any good-sized branches, pick them up. We might need them. That sound good to you, Dietrick?"

"Options being limited, that sounds like the best approach to me."

They pressed forward. Sometimes Theresa bent for a branch. Other times it was Harper picking up branches that looked like they'd make for good walking staffs.

"Are they still following us?" Isaac asked.

After a moment: "Yes."

"We need to stop," he announced. He needed to see what they were up against. They set Emily down. "Make some noise," Isaac said.

The others stamped their feet, clapped their hands, and called out, "Hey now" and "Get!"

"This will just be for a moment," Isaac said. Then, he turned off his headlamp. After his eyes adjusted to the sudden darkness, he scanned the mist hovering low off the ground between the trees. He counted a dozen pair of curious eyes. None were blue.

Popping the snap on his belt case, he handed the buck knife to Harper. Taking a branch from her, he held it toward the ground. He showed her how to shave off the smaller branches by holding the blade at an angle and pressing it down the shaft of the branch. "Can you do this while we walk? We might need these as weapons."

"Are you thinking like a quarter staff or more of a boar spear? I could whittle a point at the end of each."

Her question was in earnest. He smiled despite their circumstances, recalling how he'd heard the girls talk that way when they would play Dungeons and Dragons. "Whatever you think best," he said.

The towering image of the bipedal canine came into his mind like a sudden nightmare. His pants and underwear were still damp from when he'd pissed himself. He could smell the bacterial stench of the creature's fur lingering in his nostrils. His smile faded. "Let's try to pick up the pace until we get to the road," he said, though he wasn't really certain that the road would be safer.

They continued with very little talking between them. Isaac would ask if they were still being followed, and someone would confirm that the coyotes were keeping pace, though at a cautious distance. Isaac said a quiet prayer for the battery in his headlamp. He'd asked Dietrick to test his flashlight, and it was dead. Their journey was accompanied by the intermittent strick and skitch of Harper removing smaller twigs from the branches in her hands.

Isaac looked back over his shoulder at Emily laid out on the stretcher. She was pale, mouth agape. Her slow, rhythmic breathing barely moved her ribs. He turned back to the trail revealing itself at the edges of his plodding light. The way she lay reminded him of a painting he'd seen in his younger days. He couldn't get the image of it out of his mind.

In college, Gwen had talked him into a Humanities elective called Painters and Poets. In it, they'd studied paintings influenced by poems and poems influenced by paintings. Much of the course was lost to him in the mysteries of fickle memory. He'd be the first to admit that he hadn't tried all that hard to remember much of it. If it had meant spending time with Gwen, he could be talked into just about anything.

He'd forgotten the poet, but the poem was about the Lady of Shalott—a noblewoman cursed to live in a tower, weaving into a tapestry what she can see of the world by looking into a mirror aimed out her window. Her mysterious curse kept her from engaging with the world directly. The road to distant, downstream Camelot passes right past her window, and in time she sees Lancelot in her mirror's reflection. She falls instantly in love. "Half-sick of shadows" (he still remembered that line), she resolved herself to pursue Lancelot. Despite the curse, she leaves her tower, takes a boat from the shore, and floats down the river towards the towers of Camelot. Traveling in a storm, she freezes to death, proving the veracity of the curse. The poem ends with the people of Camelot seeing her corpse floating past the banks of the city.

"Jesus," he recalled goading Gwen, "these poets were sure a happy-go-lucky bunch, weren't they?"

Many painters had depicted the image of the Lady of Shalott dead in her boat as she drifted on the stream. She lay prone and pale, much like his daughter on the litter behind him.

He trudged forward. Flanked by coyotes and marching the endless path toward a vague destination, he felt lost. Anything you have here, Gwen. It's been over a decade, and I still don't know what the hell I'm doing with our kids. If there's any way you can help me, I'll take it, he thought.

His headlamp flickered and then flashed out. The dark washed over them.

"Perfect," he muttered. He then turned toward the inhaled noises of concern behind him. "We'll be okay, don't worry. The road's gotta be close, and the moon is bright enough that we'll be able to see once our eyes adjust. I can already see the—hold on."

A hum in the distance grew into the drone of an approaching vehicle.

"Hey!" Carson shouted. "Stop! We're here. Help!"

Headlight flashed through the trees in front of them as a southbound vehicle drove down Tin Shanty Bridge Road. Its tires crunched over dirt and whatever debris hadn't been cleared from the ground.

"Over here!" Harper yelled.

"They're moving at a clip," Isaac said.

Carson, Harper, and Theresa jumped up and down, waving their arms and shouting.

"Over here!" Dietrick yelled.

The headlights passed them and then, to their left through the trees, they watched the red of the taillights slowly wink out through the trunks and distance.

"Come back!" Carson shouted in one final Hail Mary attempt to get the driver's attention.

Save for the fading sound of the vehicle's engine, the woods were silent. Then:

"Carson?"

Carson turned from the direction of the vehicle's disappearance back to the direction from which it had appeared. "Carly?"

Bow and arrow still in hand, he took off at a bolt down the half-light of the trail.

"Carson!" Isaac called after him but knew that it was futile. Scanning the woods, he saw that the coyotes were gone, likely spooked by the vehicle or the shouting. Or both. He looked back at Dietrick. "Got it in you to double-time it?"

Dietrick nodded.

In short time, they emerged from the overhead cover of the trail out onto the road. The landscape around them was largely black and white with a slightly bluish tincture. To the north, some twenty yards from them, the light of the full moon made a silhouette of Carson and Carly where they stood holding each other in a tight embrace in the middle of the road. Another slightly taller silhouette stood just off to the left of them.

Isaac and the others approached. He and Dietrick lowered Emily to the ground.

"They found each other," Isaac said to Morgan. He nodded toward Carson and Carly still entwined.

Morgan shook her head. "She hasn't shut up about him." She looked at Emily on the stretcher and then around to the faces of the others. "You've made friends."

Dietrick stepped forward and introduced himself as a forest ranger. Isaac made the other introductions. While Harper tended to Emily and tried to get her to drink, Isaac took Morgan to the side. A mix of truth and lie, he brought her up to speed on the surprise visit and Emily's subsequent "seizure" after the storm. He talked about Theresa as Emily's aunt, and then he explained half-truths about the tragedy of Zara, whom he called Theresa's roommate.

"Her lover then?" Morgan said.

Isaac looked at Theresa and then back to Morgan. "That's never been said specifically, but I've always guessed it." He surprised himself with his ability to lie. "She's still in shock, so we're trying not to talk about it."

Morgan nodded. "Emily's aunt? So, she's your sister?"

Isaac shook his head. "Old friend of the family on my wife's side. They've always called her Aunt Theresa. I really don't know the whole story."

"Have you seen a young man?" Dietrick called over to Morgan. "He'd be about your age, dressed like me?"

"We haven't seen anybody," Morgan said. "Just the asshole in that last car who didn't even slow down as we waved like idiots at him from the shoulder."

She then filled them in on what had happened with her and Carly. After they'd dropped Carson off at the dispersed campsite, they came back out this way and took Tin Shanty Bridge Road up toward Cornwall Lake. "They have an elk viewing area up there, too." She looked over at Carly and Carson sitting on a log, holding hands, and speaking quietly to each other. "She really wanted to see an elk, so I figured I'd give it one more go."

"It's isolated," Dietrick said, ever the knowledgeable ranger. "It tends to be a good spot."

"Well, good or no, we didn't see anything. The storm came through, but up there by the lake, it was just a heavy downpour that we waited out in the car."

Isaac nodded. "You missed a doozy." He told her about his truck.

"Not nearly that bad, but we had a mishap with our car, too." She shook her head and smiled bitterly. "I was so fired up to get these two, and then just her, to see an elk that I wasn't really paying attention. We ran out of gas on the way back before we even hit Lost Lakes Road."

"You were up there a ways," Dietrick said.

She nodded. "We stayed with the car for a bit, figuring we could flag someone down, but the storm must have really shut down traffic. We didn't see anybody until that guy going by that you just saw." She shrugged. "We both fell asleep in the car, and when we woke up in the dark, we started walking."

"Did you drop off to sleep instantly?" Dietrick asked.

Morgan offered him a puzzled look. "It was just a nap."

Isaac touched Dietrick's shoulder and gave it a slight squeeze as if to intuit, "Hey, we don't need to scare anybody with that story."

Dietrick seemed to get the message and changed the subject. "Well, you are welcome to continue with us. You'd have a heck of a time trying to get back to your campsite right now. If the pop-up is yours, it's okay. Not a scratch." He smiled. "We are going to stick to the road and head back to the ranger station."

Morgan looked toward her sister. "Carly?"

"Yes. We're going with them."

Morgan smiled resignedly.

Isaac nodded. In just over an hour, they'd be at the Witness Tree.

CHAPTER 17

The full moon lit their way on the road, giving them the same visibility they would have had if it were dusk. Tin Shanty Bridge Road stretched out in front of them to the north like a stagnant, gray river cutting through the darkness. He checked in the east, but Isaac wasn't certain if it was getting any closer to daybreak. Nobody among them had a way to get accurate time.

Someone had come through with a chainsaw and cleared most of the fallen trees obstructing the road. They'd rolled the sheared logs onto the sandy shoulder. Other than avoiding the large puddles, their travels were largely unhindered.

They followed Tin Shanty Bridge Road north to Sturgeon Valley and then took the new road west. Though Sturgeon Valley had almost no blowdown with only a few snags in the surrounding trees, the road itself rose and fell with hills. Everyone talked less as they trudged up the hills and then, in silence, enjoyed the reprieve of the declines. Isaac played out in his head the various ways he might approach bringing up the Witness Tree. There was no explaining it without explaining it truthfully, and explaining it truthfully seemed to beg to be disbelieved. In moments as they walked, with the darkness of the woods on either side of them, their collective labored breathing, and his arms aching with the weight of the stretcher, the idea of stopping at the Witness Tree struck him as absurd.

In less than an hour, they'd be at Twin Lakes Road. From there, it was another mile or so to the ranger station. How would they not be just as safe there? They could have coffee. They could dry out their shoes and socks. He could come to his senses and have someone drive him and Emily into the Gaylord hospital to have her checked out.

No, instead he was going to take refuge at a tree. What they were supposed to do once they arrived at the tree was unknown, seemingly even to Theresa, who insisted that the tree was their destination.

He glanced back at her, puffing along to keep up with them—looking, as always, homeless—hunched and leaning her weight on a branch that she'd turned into a walking stick. She didn't look like the kind of person from whom one would take advice. Then again, there wasn't anything ordinary about what they were experiencing.

"We're getting close," Dietrick said, as though reading Isaac's thoughts. "When we get to Twin Lakes Road, we might even be fortunate enough to get a ride to the station."

"Stay the course," a woman's voice spoke clearly.

Isaac looked over his shoulder. "What?"

Morgan gave him a puzzled look. "Nobody said anything."

Behind her, Carson and Carly were walking, hand in hand, their heads leaned into each other, quietly whispering.

Isaac turned his head back to the road. A sign on the shoulder indicated that the next turnout to their right would lead them down to see the Witness Tree.

"Stay the course." Hearing it again, whispered into his ear this time, he couldn't deny that it sounded like Gwen speaking to him. He stopped in a pool of moonlight coming through the break in the tree canopy above the intersection of the road and the northbound two-track.

"Not here," Dietrick said, "but we are getting close."

Isaac cleared his throat. "Dietrick, trade off with someone."

"I'm not sure—"

"I'll do it," Harper said.

Isaac felt the jostle of the stretcher as Harper took the back polls from Dietrick.

Dietrick walked up to Isaac's side. "I don't understand." He gestured toward the two-track. "This goes down to the Witness Tree."

"I know," Isaac said. "You're welcome to continue to the ranger station. You probably should." He turned the front of the litter so he could see the others. "Morgan, you and your sister should probably go with Dietrick."

"I'm going wherever Carson is going," Carly said.

Morgan looked at her sister's hand, the fingers of which were braided tightly into Carson's fingers. She shrugged. "Looks like we're going with you...if that's okay."

Dietrick reached up and scratched behind his ear. "I still don't—"

"You don't need to understand," Theresa snapped. "We are taking Emily to The Witness Tree. We are done talking about it."

Dietrick was quiet for a moment, seemingly searching each of their faces for an explanation. "Okay, then. I'll remain with you," he said. "Splitting up is never the answer in situations like this." He reached behind his head to tighten the band on his ponytail. "I would want the record to reflect, however, that I was opposed to this detour."

"What record?" Morgan said. "What are you even talking about?"

"I meant figuratively. I would be remiss if I didn't inform the group that the—"

"Ready, Harper?" Isaac interrupted, ignoring their argument.

"Yes."

They trudged down the two-track that soon opened out into a parking area where tourists could park their cars at a split-rail fence. From there, they could walk the rest of the hiking trail to the Witness Tree. The full moon lit their way. After a few more minutes of walking, the trail spread out into an earthen clearing. In the middle of the clearing, Isaac spotted the black, rectangular silhouette of the wooden Department of Natural Resources sign with etched lettering that explained the significance of the tree as a survey marker. Behind the sign, the silhouette of the tree itself shot straight skyward toward the moon. No limbs protruded from the first thirty feet of the red pine. Beyond that, gnarled branches twisted outward from the trunk.

Isaac looked at Theresa. "What now?"

Theresa craned her neck, tracing her eyes up the height of the tree. After a moment, she turned her head toward Isaac. "Set her down at the base."

Isaac and Harper walked Emily to the tree and then lowered her down among its exposed roots.

"Okay," Isaac said. "Now what?"

"We wait."

"Wait? Are you saying that you don't know what we're—"

Dietrick cleared his throat. "I really need to know what this is all about."

"There's something here with us...something evil," Theresa said.

"Look!" Harper pointed.

In the darkness among the trees that encircled the Witness Tree clearing, a pair of electric blue eyes hovered, slowly stalking a circle around them.

Isaac's heart raced in his ribcage. "Oh, shit...Theresa, it's that wiindi—it's that fucking thing."

Harper picked up one of the makeshift spears, took it in both hands, and stood trembling over Emily.

"Carly, you have to let go," Carson said. He was trying to get his left hand on his bow and his right fingers around the nock of the arrow.

Carly clung to him. "I'm scared, Carson. Just do as I...just listen to me. I'm scared."

Morgan stood with her eyes closed, lips mumbling.

Carson stopped struggling against Carly's clinging.

Isaac bent and then picked up two spears from the ground. "Dietrick," he called. When Dietrick looked his way, Isaac tossed a spear to him.

Dietrick caught it, looked at it a moment, and then looked back to Isaac. "What am I supposed to do with—"

A hulking, hairy shadow shot out of the darkness and across the clearing. Its feet and hands tore up chunks of earth as it ran. A startled exhale left Dietrick's lips as the form lifted him from the ground and carried him into the blackness of the woods. His spear lay on the ground near to where he'd stood.

Dietrick shrieked. His dying cry was followed by the sounds of rending flesh, snapped bones, and a ravenous, feasting growl.

Harper screamed.

Everything of Isaac's sight dissolved instantly to black. The spear pulled from his grip, ripped into the blackness. He staggered, reaching his hands out in front of him. He knew his eyes were open, but he may as well have been inside a closed coffin for all he could see.

"Dad?" Carson called. The teen's voice faded out quickly as though he were falling down a deep well.

Isaac tried to answer, but no words left his mouth. He flailed and stumbled around what he had to believe was still the clearing. None of his movements, not even his shuffling feet, made a noise in the crushing silence.

Cold lips spoke frosted words into his ear. "Stop moving. Just listen," the male voice whispered.

Isaac's ear felt numb. He recognized the voice. It was the same voice that had confronted the mangey coyote in the den beneath the cabin. Isaac passed his arm blindly through a column of cold. His larynx, tongue, teeth and lips rebelled against his attempts at speech.

"For now," the voice whispered into his other ear, "just listen, and you will understand why you have come under the shadow of my height and breadth."

Isaac felt more like he was floating than standing. If he concentrated, he could feel, just vaguely, the contact between the soles of his shoes and the ground.

"Yes," the voice said, in answer to Isaac's thought but unasked question. "You will be able to speak once I make my inquiries."

The whispering, though indiscernible, voices of what sounded like dozens of women soundtracked the stygian void.

"Do you come here of your own freewill?" the male voice asked.

Isaac felt a salivary click at the back of his throat, unleashing the biological mechanics of speech. "What? I'm here because—"

"Please just answer yes or no. Do you come here of your own freewill?"

"What is happening? That thing...my kids—"

"They are unharmed. You can trust me. You only need tell me if you come here of—"

"I'm not even sure where I am."

Silence. Then: "To the Witness Tree. Do you come to us—to me—of your own freewill?"

"I'm bringing my daughter to—"

"Now is not a time for obstinance."

"Yes, then, for Christ's sake."

"Yes?"

"Yes, I come here of my own freewill. I'm here because—"

"And you make this father's sacrifice willingly?"

The whispering of the women went on around him like the buzzing of a hornet's nest. Fingers touched lightly over him, moved him, like someone holding something up to the light for a better look.

"Father's sacrifice?" he asked, dizzy with the way he felt he was being turned and examined.

"Do you make it willingly?"

Isaac thought for a moment. "Where is everybody?"

"They are with you, and you will see them again. Soon. Time is not on our side. Do you make this father's sacrifice willingly?"

Isaac felt the cold twisting around him like a knot of pythons. Around his wrists, his ankles. Was he kneeling? Theresa had received a dream. So had Madame Zara. In the dream, the Witness Tree had spoken to them, even beckoned them. Told them that this was the only way to save Emily. The tree had spoken and was likely speaking to him. If so, the tree had saved him from the skinwalker. Theresa had offered her own opinion about the entity behind the voice: "It feels we have something on our side," she'd said. What was it about Isaac that made him doubt everything? They'd reached the tree. They were safe. They were—

Don't.

Gwen's voice came into his head as plain as his thoughts. She sounded strained, as though trying to speak through the onset of anesthesia.

Doubt.

"I have asked a question that will not be asked again," the tree said, with a growing bite to his voice.

What did Isaac know? Theresa, Madame Zara—hell, even Gwen—were much more sensitive to these mysteries. He'd been wrong or obtuse too many times in the past. His brother had died because he'd taken them to that goddamn island.

"I make this father's sacrifice willingly," he blurted, as Gwen's final word came into his mind.

Yourself.

The darkness fell from around him, dissolving to the blue-lit clearing. Even the moon's soft, reflected light was too much for his dilated pupils. He made to bury his face in the crook of his elbow, but something restrained his arms behind him. Instead, he closed his eyes and waited for his pupils to adjust. Like lightning preceding thunder, his sight came back to him before his hearing.

Soon he heard them. Harper wept quietly, calling out for "Mr. Fletcher." Theresa's voice came from somewhere above with a repeated refrain: "I'm sorry. I'm so sorry. I didn't know."

"I didn't know," Carly repeated mockingly. She laughed.

"Carly," Morgan said. "Act your age."

Isaac blinked and squinted. "What's going on?" His eyes had finally adjusted enough that he found focus. He looked down at himself. Shirtless, he kneeled at the base of a tree with his back pressed up against it. His arms were behind him around the trunk. His wrists were lashed tightly together. His ankles were bound similarly. As he pulled at his restraints, the bark of the tree worked against the skin of his arms like sandpaper.

Twenty feet in front of him, head lolled to the side on her neck, Emily was held upright against the trunk of the Witness Tree, bound with vine and ivy. Rivulets of blood ran down her thighs.

Tied to the posts that held up the DNR sign, Harper struggled against her own binding.

"I'm sorry, Isaac! I'm sorry!" Theresa shouted.

He turned his gaze skyward and spotted her, dangling upside down some twenty-five feet in the air. Her hat had fallen from her head and lay on the ground beneath her. Hog-tied at the ankles and suspended by vine from one of the lowest branches of the Witness Tree, she flailed her arms uselessly. "Say nothing else, Isaac!"

"Oh, do guide him, wise Virgil," Carly said, standing next to her sister in the middle of the clearing. "Perhaps you'll have another dream. Surely the *tree* will tell you what to do." She chortled.

With his gaze skyward, Isaac saw a whorl of bats circling in the air above the clearing. Theresa screamed for help with everything her lungs had to give.

"Enough," Morgan said. She raised her hand, opening her fingers and then slowly closing them into a fist.

Detritus rose up from the ground twisting into a small tornado that corkscrewed up into Theresa's mouth, stuffing it with leaves. Morgan opened her fist, and the remaining leaves and twigs fluttered to the ground.

Isaac blinked, noticing his son for the first time since emerging from the darkness. "Carson? What are you doing?"

Carson stepped up to Carly's side. He gripped his bow's riser in his left hand while the fingers of his right hand twitched around the string just beneath the fletching of the nocked arrow.

Carly looked at Carson. "This man is threatening. Protect me."

Wordless, Carson raised his bow, drew the string back, and took aim at his father's chest. A tear broke from his eye and slid over his cheek.

"Carly," Morgan said flatly. "If he accidentally kills him…"

Carly smiled at Isaac where he kneeled bound to the tree. "Fine. Lower your weapon, darling."

Carson did as instructed, though he kept his hands on the riser and string, at the ready.

"What a gift you've brought me," Carly said. "Such a handsome familiar."

Isaac looked at his mesmerized boy, and then his skinny, pale daughter bound to the Witness Tree. "What are you… Morgan? Emily isn't well. I don't understand what—"

"You don't understand?" The sound that came out of her could be called a laugh, though it was lifeless. "You must remember Evelyn, our sister?" She motioned toward herself and Carly. "You injected poison into her bloodstream… not an act one would soon forget." She stared at him for a moment. "Your gape-mouthed expression suggests that you are beginning to understand your predicament and your culpability."

Isaac blinked. "Your sist...Evelyn? Your sister?" The image of her writhing on her bed of branches as the lampricide coursed through her veins played in his mind. Behind Morgan, the blue, menacing eyeshine loomed again in the darkness of the surrounding trees. The eyes steadily moved closer.

"She was trying to take Emily from me. Silas—" Isaac swallowed. "Morgan, whatever this is..." he started. Shuddering, he looked again at the approaching eyes. "We aren't safe here. There's something...you aren't safe—"

"They have no reason to fear me." Branson Strang's voice preceded him as he stepped out of the woods into the light of the clearing. His glimmering eyes settled themselves into the canvas of his face. "Like yours to you, they are my children." Striding fully into view, he was towering and naked, though somewhat obscured by a thick covering of body hair. Dried blood covered his chin and wooly chest. His large phallus hung low, wreathed by a thick nest of pubic hair.

"Ranger Strang?" Isaac asked weakly.

In his left arm, Strang held a wide-eyed, whimpering baby. "Shh. Shh," he cooed, kissing the child on its cheek. "Be still."

The baby quieted and then rested its small head against the stringy hair of Strang's shoulder.

Pulling futilely against her binding, Harper sobbed openly.

Carly ratcheted her fingers and thumb in the air, her hand gesturing like a stalking spider. "Quiet," she said.

Harper slumped to sleep instantly.

Isaac stared at Strang standing with the dozing baby. His mind went to the abandoned stroller they'd found. "How do you have...what are you...?"

"I know your musk," Morgan said. "I smelled it on that cursed syringe. I smell it now. I've waited so long to bring pain into your life."

Carly stepped in front of Isaac. Smiling, she spoke with Gwen's voice. "Stay the course," she whispered mockingly. Then, she laughed before breaking off from the group. She walked across the clearing and stepped into the darkness of the surrounding trees.

Isaac looked at a dead-eyed Carson and then to Emily lashed to the Witness Tree. Her head lolled to the left and then to the right. She moaned softly.

Isaac glared into Morgan's eyes. "If you touch my kids, bitch...if you lay—"

"What?" Strang said, "so much as a finger on them?" He raised his free hand into the air. "Save the cliches and make no mistake as to who has power here and who is powerless." He squeezed his hand into a fist until one of his knuckles cracked. The sound was answered instantly by the snap of the vine holding Theresa upside down high above the ground. Her descending scream was muffled. Leaves trailed from her falling mouth. The cracking of her neck against the ground was like a branch being broken over someone's knee.

"I think we've had enough of wannabe Indians, don't you?"

Isaac winced, turning his head away from the lifeless body.

"Between having magic and having none, I find the worse off are those with just a touch of the gift. Theresa. Zara. They know just enough to make fools of themselves." Strang smiled. "Although they can prove useful at times. Blind leading the blind, and all that."

Isaac opened his eyes. He looked up into Strang's face. His voice cracked. "I just need to know what you want. I'll do it. Just tell me what—"

"You've already done what I want." He stroked his free hand over the sleeping baby. "You came here of your own freewill." He gestured his hand toward Emily. "You have willingly made your father's sacrifice so *my* child might yet live again. You have only one more sacrifice to make, but it will be no skin off your teeth, as they say. Not off your teeth." He smiled. "We just need a baby blanket from you."

Isaac shook his bewildered head. "What...I don't..."

Carly emerged into the clearing carrying a shallow baby basket woven from branches and lined with fresh fern leaves. She stepped up to Strang who then used both hands to lower the baby into the waiting basket.

Carly walked to the Witness Tree. She laid the basket with sleeping baby at Emily's feet. The full moon shined down on all of it. Carly gripped Emily's face in her left hand until Emily's eyes drifted open. "Do you see me, Evelyn? It's time, sister. Your homecoming."

Isaac thrusted forward against the restraint of the vines. He might as well have been trying to break free of a straitjacket. "I'm going to kill you...you motherfuckers...I'm going to..."

Strang waved his hand across the air in front of him, like a priest offering a blessing.

Isaac could no longer speak.

"What do you think you could possibly do to me on this soil that hasn't already been done? What pain could you possibly inflict that I haven't already endured fivefold? I was standing here, just a boy, when those thugs from Wolverine shot my father in cold blood. Shot him for simply saying no. He refused to take his people from this land that rightfully belonged to him, meager as it was." He shook his head. "My father's blood watered the roots of that tree before they set him on fire." He pointed to the Witness Tree. "My father is the tree. The tree is my father. This is our land and will always be our land."

Strang stepped closer to Isaac. He lifted his face by the chin. "You're not going to do anything to us. You've already caused us so much loss. You can't save your children but, then again, they were never yours. Not really."

Isaac's eyes widened. The squalls of adrenaline and shock were too much to call what was going through his head thoughts. His mind was a storm.

Fading slowly into consciousness, Emily moaned and whimpered.

Strang smiled, almost sympathetically. "You are a wellspring, Isaac. A carrier. You have no gifts yourself but, when well-matched, you sire those with potential. To be sure, your first born disappointed us. Without gifts, like her father. Your youngest exhibited some clairaudience, if not clairsentience, though he seems to have largely outgrown it. But your Emily, the prize," he said, gesturing behind him toward the Witness Tree, "made all the monitoring and manipulation worth it. She hums with the gift, but she has preserved Evelyn's spirit long enough."

He studied Isaac's face as he writhed against his binding. He leaned in closer and whispered. "You have to be able to feel in your heart that a woman of Gwen's caliber, of her intelligences, would never have been with you of her own free—" Strang released Isaac's chin and took a step back from his convulsing and attempted headbutting. "That's right. Get it out. It's a lot to take in to learn that everything you lived was a lie." He smiled and leaned in again to whisper: "I want your final realization to be that your wife never really loved you... not of her own accord."

Emily moaned louder. "Don't..." she murmured.

Strang looked back at her. "We're close," he said, looking to Morgan and Carly.

Isaac slumped his head back against the tree, turning his gaze from Strang toward the woods. A half dozen sets of eyes glowed white with a tinge of yellow in the trees to their east. Given the distance of the eyeshine from the ground, the animals were much taller than coyotes. What the hell was it... an army of wiindigoo?

"I can see you, sisters," Emily mumbled.

"Father," Morgan said. "It's time. The veil is thinned."

Strang smiled. "I know you're anxious, Morgan. You've waited too long to revel in his pain. Too long to know your revenge."

She glared at Isaac. "Silas was my son."

Isaac swallowed.

Strang retreated backwards to the Witness Tree. He kneeled first to the sleeping baby. "Soon, my little Evelyn," he said towards the sky as much as toward the baby. "Soon." He then stood and stroked Emily's hair, whispering something into her ear.

"No," Emily moaned.

Isaac thrashed again until Morgan stepped in front of him, obscuring his view of the Witness Tree. She reached down to his belt, flipped the snap, and drew his buck knife out. Opening it, she turned the shiny blade back and forth in front of her face. "Good, it's dull," she said, smiling. "I want you to feel this in the worst way." She stared into Isaac's eyes. "I'm sure you've wondered what your brother's last moments were like. You're about to live them." Without turning from Isaac, she spoke again, but her words were directed toward Strang. "I need to hear him, Father."

"Of course," Strang said. A knuckle cracked in his hand.

Isaac felt his power of speech returned.

Morgan set the tip of the blade against the flesh of Isaac's shoulder joint. "I'll be the first to admit that I don't have my son's flaying skills." A drop of blood slid down Isaac's chest from the beginning of the piercing. He winced and then wailed when she suddenly leaned her weight into the blade, plunging the sharp of the knife into the soft space just beneath his collar bone.

"Beautiful," Carly said, stepping closer. Carson stayed back, guarding her rear.

Strang clamped his palm over Emily's mouth, pushing the back of her skull into the tree. A rhythmic chanting emanated from his throat.

"Leave her alone, you sonuvabitch!" Isaac shouted.

Carly moaned from her throat. "Slowly, Morgan. Make him suffer."

Blood streamed down Isaac's chest as she sawed the blade through his skin in the motion he might use to gut a large fish. Carly gasped in a pleasurable breath.

The knife blade felt as though it had been set aflame as Morgan cut a gash across the horseshoe of bone at the top of his sternum. "Fuck! Fuck!" Isaac shouted. "You fucking bitch!"

Emily struggled to wrench her mouth free of Strang's hand.

"Okay," Carson said, his voice both trembling and resolute. "I will."

Carly snapped her fierce eyes on him. "Carson, who are you talking to?"

He turned and in one fluid motion raised his bow while drawing the string.

"You don't have him, you stupid little tramp!" Morgan shouted, turning from her work of skinning Isaac.

Carson released the arrow. Shot through the throat, Strang emitted a sound akin to a dog stumbling into a sand hornet's nest. He reeled backwards, clawing at the arrow sticking out of his neck, a blood-choked howl gurgled from his larynx. Carly and Morgan rushed toward him. With Strang's palm no longer over her mouth, Emily roared until the guttural release became words. Her deafening volume was otherworldly: "You leave my father alone!"

As though summoned, dozens of elk stampeded out of the trees and into the clearing as though water rushing from a breached dam. Like something sucked down a drain, Carly disappeared in the trampling storm of dust and bodies and legs...the beginning of her scream snuffed instantly to silence. A bull elk lifted Morgan from the ground in its massive rack. It tossed her into the air, and when she came down again the tines of its antlers punctured through her ribs and lower back. Her mouth screamed soundlessly. The ground thundered with hammering hooves. The earth shook. Carson stood still and pale in the center of all of it. The herd slipped around him, like water past a boulder in the river.

It was the last hazy image Isaac saw before his head slumped forward onto his bleeding chest, and he faded into unconsciousness.

CHAPTER 18

A dull pain smoldered along the skin just under Isaac's collar bone. His eyes slowly fluttered open. His back was still against the tree, but his arms and legs were no longer bound. Harper kneeled at his side. To the east, the trees were beginning to lighten with the coming of the sun.

"You're okay, Mr. Fletcher," she said. "We're here."

He shifted his shoulder and then winced at the sting of pain from his chest. The wound itself was closed. It looked as though it'd been healing for a few days. On the ground to Harper's right was a small pile of blood-soaked sanitary napkins. On the sleeping bag behind her, Emily lay with her eyes closed and her knees pulled up to her chest.

"How long have I been out?" Isaac asked. Somebody had balled up his shirt and put it between his bare back and the tree.

"A few hours," Harper said.

He looked at the sanitary napkins. A bloody t-shirt lay not far from them. "Is she—"

"The blood is from you," Harper said. "She's okay." She held a water bottle up to his lips. "Here, try to take a drink."

Lukewarm or no, the water went down his throat like an elixir. He took the bottle from her with his right hand. He took a longer drink.

"I packed the sanitary napkins into the deeper parts of your cut. It's the only way I could get the bleeding to stop."

He set the back of his head against the tree. He closed his eyes. The memories of what had happened came to him. He felt the knife again as though it were still slicing through him. He opened his eyes. The clearing gave away little that had happened, save for the divots of earth from the elks' hooves. Strang was gone. No trace of Morgan nor Carly's bodies either. Not far from the Witness Tree, Theresa's trampled body lay in a crumpled heap.

"Where's Carson?" Isaac asked with sudden panic in his voice.

Harper twisted the cap back onto the water bottle. "He walked back out to the road. He said he wanted to see if he could flag somebody down."

Looking at it, Isaac touched his fingers along the healing wound. "How did you..."

"Emily healed you. All I did was stop the bleeding."

He looked at her. "How did you know how to do that...stop the bleeding, I mean?"

She exhaled a small, disbelieving laugh from her nose. "I'm going to school for nursing. How do you not know that, Mr. Fletcher?" She looked at the ground. "Sorry, that was probably rude."

He shook his head. "No, it's okay. I should know that. I'm sorry." He looked at Emily. "She's good?"

"I'm okay, Dad," Emily said without opening her eyes. "I just need to rest. That was a lot."

Harper crawled over to Emily. She lifted her head, so it pillowed on Harper's thigh. She stroked her hand over Emily's damp hair.

Isaac smiled at the sight of them. Tears welled along his eyes. He took a deep breath. It felt like the first he'd taken in days. "You girls," he started. "I want to help you girls. I can give you the money for some of the starter costs on an apartment. I can help you buy pots and pans and stuff."

Emily smiled in her dozing. "Thanks, Dad. And you don't have to worry—"

"I'm not worried about the money," Isaac interrupted. "I know you're ready."

Emily opened her eyes. "I know I'm ready too...at least ready to try." She smiled sympathetically. "But I'm talking about you. You don't have to worry about you. We won't leave you by yourself. You won't ever be alone."

A tear broke from his eye. Had she just synthesized all of his troubled thoughts into one overarching fear? Would they each in turn grow up and walk away without much reason to look back? Would his phone stop ringing? Would the front door stop opening and closing? Maybe what he feared was ending up a ghost in his old age, haunting a house of half-memories and lost emotions. Emily was telling him that wouldn't be his fate. She wasn't going to leave him, even if she moved out.

She smiled. "You okay, Dad?"

He nodded, sniffing in a breath. "I think so." He returned her smile. "Happy birthday, Em."

She closed her eyes. "Oh, that's right. I'd forgotten."

Footsteps approached on the path behind Isaac. He pressed his palms to the ground as though to push himself up on the way to standing. He winced.

"It's okay," Harper said. "It's just Carson."

"We need to move from here as soon as we can," Carson called before even reaching them. "This is blighted land... profane ground."

"Carson?"

Carson stepped into Isaac's view. In his left arm he held the sleeping baby. In his right, one of the sharpened spears. "I'm just telling you what I'm being told."

Emily kept her eyes closed. "I should be able to walk in a few more minutes."

Carson let his spear fall out of his hand to the ground. He crouched down to kneel in front of his father. "How are you doing, Dad?"

Isaac reached his hand out and set it on Carson's knee. "I've been better, but I'm good right now." He smiled.

Carson stroked the palm of his free hand from Isaac's temple to his cheek where he let it rest a moment. He waited until Isaac looked into his eyes. "It's not true, Dad. What that asshole said to you about Mom. Mom says it's not true. She loves you. She always did." His eyes looked off to the left, as though he were listening. He nodded slightly. "And she says it's okay about *Walden*. She says it's not an easy book. Stick to the Hemingway, she says."

Isaac's lips buckled in against his teeth, and another tear broke from his eye. "Tell her...tell her that I love—"

Carson shook his head. "She's not here anymore, Dad. She had to go. But she knows." He smiled sympathetically. "Uncle Adam, too. He says he does forgive you. Or better still that there was nothing to forgive. He says to tell you that he has to go...all the way home. He says you'll know what that means."

Tears streamed from Isaac's eyes. He stared into Carson's. "How did you...I thought Carly had taken your mind...I thought..."

Carson reached into his pocket. When he brought his hand out again, he showed Isaac three iron nails in his palm. "Zara gave these to me when we were driving back to the campsite. She said they'd protect me. When we were getting close to the Witness Tree, Mom told me to just pretend to do what Carly was saying. She told me she'd tell me what to do and when."

Isaac nodded. "You did good." He looked at Harper stroking Emily's hair. "You all did so good. You saved me. You saved us."

The sun continued its gradual rising. The baby in Carson's arms cooed peacefully in its sleep.

CHAPTER 19

Pacing the small room, Ben held the baby against his chest. She looked so diminutive in her swaddling blanket and hat. Ashley smiled sleepily from the bed, watching them. She shook her head, amused. "It's like she wanted to be born on Emily's birthday. That is going to be one excited little aunt."

Ben smiled into the tiny face. "Little Gwendoline." He then looked at Ashley. "Are you sure your dad is going to be okay with us naming her that? Like it won't be too much?"

She nodded. "I think he'll be thrilled." She scootched herself up against her stack of pillows. "What time is it?"

Ben walked over to the visitor's chaise lounge. His phone sat on the arm of the chair. He tapped the screen, and its small rectangle of light glowed into the room. "Almost three o'clock in the morning."

Ashley reached out, beckoning for little baby Gwen with her fingers. An intravenous line dangled from her arm. "Let me hold her again."

Ben smiled. "But I just got her." He walked her over to Ashley, despite his half-hearted protest.

Ashley gathered Gwedoline against her chest and kissed her on top of the hat. "We'll call my dad in the morning to tell him about someone's early arrival. He and Carson were supposed to get back from fishing yesterday."

Gwendoline fussed restlessly in her sleep, growing in agitation. Then, she arched her back, writhing and crying out, seemingly in pain. "What, baby? What's wrong?" Ashley asked imploringly. "Are you poked somewhere?" Two bulbs in the bathroom popped into a shower of sparks. The few lights in the main room flickered and then went out. The equipment hooked up to Ashley showed no digital readout, and the IV pump stopped its raspy breathing.

"Ben?"

"I'm on it."

Before he reached the door, everything whirred back on. Gwendoline had stopped her bawling and settled into a deep sleep again.

Hand on the doorknob, Ben looked around. "That was weird." He nibbled his lower lip. "I'm still going to get the night nurse."

"Okay," Ashley said, looking down into Gwendoline's face. "She seems fine, though...but, I mean, yeah we should tell them what just happened."

"What *did* happen?"

Ashley shrugged. "I don't know."

Ben left the room.

Ashley looked down at her fresh child's sleeping face. She closed her own eyes and lowered her head back deeper into her pillows.

Suspended over US-31, just outside the Trinity Health window, the full moon haunted the blue-black, early morning skyscape.

BIO

 J eff Vande Zande teaches fiction writing, screenwriting, and film production at Delta College in Michigan. His novels include *Into the Desperate Country* (March Street Press), *Landscape with Fragmented Figures* (Bottom Dog Press), *American Poet* (Bottom Dog Press) and *Detroit Muscle* (Whistling Shade Press). In 2012, *American Poet* won a Michigan Notable Book Award from the Library of Michigan. Montag Press released his dystopian novel, *Rules of Order*, in 2022. His gothic horror, *The Dance of Rotten Sticks*, for which *Blood of the Witness Tree* is a sequel, was released by Montag in 2024.